# Old Testament Legends

M. R. James

**Old Testament Legends**



The present edition is a reproduction of previous publication of this classic work. Minor typographical errors may have been corrected without note; however, for an authentic reading experience the spelling, punctuation, and capitalization have been retained from the original text.

ISBN: 978-1-63637-278-5

# CONTEST

## OLD TESTAMENT LEGENDS



## A THIN GHOST AND OTHERS

# OLD TESTAMENT LEGENDS

## PREFACE

If you read the title-page of this book—a thing which young persons very seldom do—you will see that it (the book) contains stories taken "out of some of the less-known apocryphal books of the Old Testament." You will very possibly not understand what that means; but if you will read this preface—another thing which young persons do even seldomer than they read a title-page—you will find the best explanation that I can give.

I have to begin by talking about the word apocryphal. The newspapers are fond of saying that a statement made by the Prime Minister (or the leader of the Opposition, according to which side in politics the newspaper takes) is apocryphal. By this, the newspaper means to say that the statement was untrue. Or, you will read that someone obtained money or goods by saying that he possessed large estates abroad; and that the estates turned out to be apocryphal. By this is meant that they did not exist. But when you read of a book being apocryphal, something rather different is meant: either that it is "spurious," i.e. that it pretends to be written by someone who did not write it; or that what is in it is fabulous and untrue, like the stories of King Arthur; or both.

Now this word apocryphal is specially used, and perhaps most often used, in connection with the Bible. Probably you have at least heard of something called "the Apocrypha," even if you have not read it, and even if you have mixed it up in your mind with another word, Apocalypse, which has nothing whatever to do with it. Well, what is "the Apocrypha"? It is to be found in many Bibles, bound up between the Old and the New Testaments. It is a set of books, looking just like the other books of the Bible, with chapters and verses. Some of it is read in church as weekday lessons in the months of October and November, as you may see by looking at the Table of Lessons in any Prayer Book. Now, are all these books of "the Apocrypha" fabulous or spurious? No. Some of them are. The

Second Book of Esdras (that is, Ezra) was not written by Ezra; The Book of Baruch (the companion of the prophet Jeremiah) was not written by Baruch; The Wisdom of Solomon was not written by Solomon. These and some others are spurious. Also, the books of Tobit and of Judith are fabulous stories. On the other hand, the book Ecclesiasticus was really written by Sirach (who is mentioned in the Preface), and The First Book of Maccabees is a true and valuable history.

Then why, if apocryphal means fabulous or spurious, or both, are these books, some of which are true and genuine, lumped all together and called "Apocrypha"? I am sorry to disappoint you, but I cannot go through the whole history. It is long, it is difficult, and though it interests me, I am inclined to think it would not interest you unless I spread it over a great many pages, and filled it out with stories; and for this I have no time. Let me tell you what strikes me as being the important thing to bear in mind. Nearly all of these books have been at some time or another read in church and treated as Scripture. Nearly all of them are now treated as Scripture by the Roman Church, but not by most of the Protestant, or Reformed, Churches. They are on the borderland of the Bible. From having been so long kept together in a group by themselves, they have come to be thought of as being all of one uniform kind. But they are not so; they are of very different sorts and merits.

Let us keep the old name for them and call them "the Apocrypha." It will be convenient to do so, because I have now to speak of other apocryphal books, which have never been bound up in our Bibles, but in older times, before Bibles were printed, were (some of them at least) read in churches and thought to be sacred books. There are a great many of these: perhaps, if they were all put together, they would make up a volume as large as the Old Testament itself; but at present there is no book in which they are all printed together. Some are stories, others are visions like those in the Revelation of St. John, others are psalms and prophecies. But all of them, I think, may fairly be called either fabulous or spurious, or both.

I can give you an example from the Bible itself to show that there were such books as long ago as the times of the Apostles, and that they were read and valued. In the 9th verse of the Epistle of Jude, you read something very curious about Satan contending with Michael about the body of Moses. Ancient writers whom we may trust tell us that this is taken from a book called The Assumption of

Moses (that is, the story of Moses being taken up out of this world at the end of his life).

We have pieces of this book still, but we have not got the whole story of the dispute between Satan and Michael. However, we know that it was represented as having taken place when Michael and the other angels were burying the body of Moses among the mountains in a place which was kept secret from all men, and that Satan said that though the soul of Moses might belong to God, the body belonged to him; and, moreover, that Moses was a murderer, because, long before, he had killed an Egyptian (as we read in Exodus ii. 12); whereupon Michael answered Satan in the words, "The Lord rebuke thee," and Satan fled. That is one example. Another is in the 14th verse of the same Epistle, where it is said that Enoch, the seventh from Adam, prophesied of the coming of the Lord to judge sinners. This verse is taken out of a long book of prophecies and visions called The Book of Enoch, which still exists, and we may read the very words in it.

In this present book, I am only concerned with the apocryphal stories; with the prophecies and visions and psalms I have nothing to do. Now, how and why did the stories come to be written?

It is likely enough that after reading some history in the Bible you may have wondered whether there was anything more to be known about the people of whom it told you. You would have liked to find out what happened to Adam, or Joseph, or David, besides the things which are written in the Bible. It was just so in ancient times —the times when our Lord was on earth, and even long before that. The Jews naturally thought a great deal about the people who are mentioned in the Old Testament; and just as there are a great many stories about the heroes of English history—such as that of King Alfred and the cakes—which, we are told now, are not true, so stories grew up about the great men of the Bible. Perhaps they were invented, some of them, in answer to questions which had been asked. Some of them were certainly made up in order to explain parts of the Bible which were difficult to understand. I will give an example of this. In the Book of Genesis (iv. 23, 24) you are told how the patriarch Lamech spoke to his wives and said, "I have slain a man to my wounding, and a young man to my hurt." Nothing is said in explanation of this; we are not told whom Lamech had killed. So a story was made up—no one knows when—which gives this explanation: Lamech was blind, and he used to amuse himself by shooting birds and beasts with bow and arrow. When he went out shooting, he used to take with him his young nephew Tubal; and Tubal used to spy the game for him and guide his hands that he might aim his arrow right. One day, when they were out together, Tubal saw, as he thought, a beast moving in the thicket; and he told Lamech, and made him aim at it, and Lamech's arrow smote the beast and killed it. But when Tubal ran to see what kind of beast it was, he found that it was not a wild beast at all. It was his ancestor Cain. For after Cain had killed Abel, and God had pronounced a curse upon him, he wandered about the earth, never able to remain in one place; and a great horn grew out of his head, and his body was covered with hair; so that Tubal, seeing him in the distance among the trunks of the trees and the brushwood, was deceived, and mistook him for a beast of chase. But when Tubal saw what had happened, he was terrified, and ran back to Lamech, crying out, "You have slain our forefather Cain!" And Lamech also was struck with horror, and raised his hands and smote them together with a mighty blow. And in so doing he struck the head of Tubal with his full strength, and Tubal fell down dead. Then Lamech returned to his house, and spoke to his wives the words that are written in the Book of Genesis. This story, a very ancient one, as I said, was invented by the Jews to explain the difficult passage in Genesis; and the early Christian writers learnt it from the Jews, and it passed into many commentaries which were written in later times; so that you may still see representations of it carved in stone in churches, both in England and elsewhere. In England it may be seen on the inside of the stone roof of Norwich Cathedral, and on the west front of Wells Cathedral; but you have to look carefully before you can find it.

There are other stories which pretend to explain texts that do not seem so difficult. For instance, in the 18th Psalm there is a verse, "Thou hast made room enough under me for to go." And about this there is a long tale of how King David went to fight the giant Ishbi-benob, and was nearly killed by him; for the giant took David and cast him to the ground, and put a heavy wine-press upon him, which would have crushed him, but that the earth beneath him suddenly became soft and yielded room for his body, and thus room was made under him.

Then again, there are others which are like parables.

At this point I will put in two short stories of the parable-kind, neither of which I think you are likely to have seen. One of them is certainly taken from an apocryphal book which is lost; and the other

I suspect to have been taken either from the same book or from one like it.

First I will tell the one about the source of which I am not certain.

In the days of King Hezekiah there was in Israel a rich man who was a miser and gave nothing to the poor. But one day it happened that he took up the book of the proverbs of King Solomon; and his eye fell upon the place where it is said, "He that hath pity upon the poor, lendeth unto the Lord; and look what he layeth out, it shall be paid him again." "So," thought he to himself, "this is a good security!" And forthwith he sold all that he had, and distributed the price among the poor, keeping for himself only two pieces of money. But, to his disappointment, he did not only become poor himself by this means, but he remained poor. The money he had given away did not come back, and no one else would give him any. So he was reduced to despair, and said, "I will go straight to Jerusalem, and demand of God why He has deceived me, and induced me to give away all my possessions by promises that are false." And he set forth. And on his way, not far from Jerusalem, he saw two men fighting, and said to them, "Brethren, what is your quarrel?" And one said, "We were journeying together, and I saw a shining stone lying in the road, and pointed it out to this man; and because he was swifter on his feet than I, he got to it first. And now he says he will keep it for himself, but I say it belongs to me, for I saw it first." Then said the traveller, "What is the value of the stone?" They said, "We do not know." And he said, "Will you take these two pieces of money for it and let me have it?" And to this they consented. So when the man got to Jerusalem, he took the stone to a jeweller and showed it to him; and no sooner had the jeweller seen it than he fell on his face and gave thanks to God. And then he said to the man, "Where did you find this? For three whole years all Jerusalem has been ransacked for this stone. Go quickly to the High Priest and give it to him, and see what he will give you!" At the same hour there came an angel to the High Priest, and said to him, "Within a few moments there will come to you a man bringing the gem which three years ago was lost out of the breastplate of Aaron the priest. Receive it at his hands, and give him for it a great sum of gold; and when you have given it, smite him lightly upon the cheek and say, 'Be not distrustful in thy heart, and slow to believe the word which says, 'He that hath pity upon the poor, lendeth unto the Lord.' For thus saith the Lord, 'Have I not now in this present world repaid thee many times over that which thou didst lend to Me? And, if thou have faith, thou shalt in the world to come receive a recompense yet many times greater than this.'" And when the man came, the High Priest did and said as he had been commanded; and the man's heart was moved, and he left in the temple all that great sum which had been given him, and for the rest of his life put his whole trust in the promises of God.

The other short story is taken out of an apocryphal book under the name of the prophet Ezekiel, and is a parable of the soul and the body of man at the day of judgment.

There was a certain king, it says, who made a marriage feast for his eldest son, and invited all his soldiers to his palace to share it. Now every one of his subjects was a soldier and served in his army, except only two, one of whom was blind and the other lame; and these two were not invited to the feast, but remained in their huts—which were near to one another—very angry and disappointed. After a while the blind man called to the lame man, "It is a shame that we are not sitting down to the feast along with the rest! I should like to treat the king as ill as he has treated us." "How can we?" said the lame man. "You know his garden," said the other; "let us go and spoil it!" "All very well," said the lame man, "but how are we to get there? I cannot walk." "Neither can I see; but we will contrive a way." So they devised a plan. The lame man plucked the grass that he could reach, and plaited it into a string, and threw one end to the blind man, who guided himself by it to the lame man. Then he took the lame man on his back, and carried him to the king's garden, and there they did all the mischief they could, trampling down and tearing up plants and flowers; and they went back to their houses and remained there. When the rest of the people came out from the banquet into the garden, they were appalled at the sight of the damage, and were much perplexed, saying, "Were not all the soldiers of the king bidden to the feast? and is not every man in the kingdom a soldier? Whence then are these tracks in the garden, and who has wrought this mischief?" After a while the king bethought him of the blind and the lame man; they were brought before him, and he said to the blind man, "Have you been into my garden?" He answered, "Alas, sire! you see my infirmity, and that I have no eyes wherewith to find my way!" Then said the king to the lame man, "And you, have you been into my garden?" And he answered, "Surely my lord has forgotten my infirmity; it cannot be that he desires to hurt my feelings by mocking me!" So the king was perplexed, and went apart to consider how the two could have contrived the business—for he was sure that they were guilty. At last a thought came to him, and he set the lame man on the blind man's shoulders, and scourged them both together. Then indeed did they cry out, and the lame said to the blind, "Did you not lend me your feet to take me to the king's garden?" And the blind to the lame, "Did you not lend me your eyes to show me the way?" And in like manner at the judgment the soul will say to the body, "I could not have sinned if you had not given me the limbs with which I did evil." And the body to the soul, "But it was you who thought of the evil which I carried out." Thus one will try to throw the blame on the other; but is either of them free from guilt?

Others of these apocryphal books are designed to show how important some special virtue, or how dangerous some particular sin, may be. Thus, there is a book called The Testaments (or Last Words) of the Twelve Patriarchs, in which each of the twelve sons of Jacob, when he comes to die, calls his children to him and tells them about his own life, and warns them against his own besetting sin, or shows how he has been helped by practising some good habit: Simeon speaks about envy, Issachar about simplicity, Zebulun about kindness, and so on. And many others there are which are merely, one would say, meant to tell us more about the lives and deaths of the great men of the old times than we can learn from the Bible.

Perhaps I have now said enough to show of what sort the tales are that are told in this book—some of them told for the first time in English. They are not true, but they are very old; some of them, I think, are beautiful, and all of them seem to me interesting. In case anyone should wish to know more about them, I will put down here the names of the books from which I have taken them.

The first part of the story of Adam is shortened from Mr. S. G.Malan's translation of The Book of Adam and Eve, and from Dillmann's German translation of the same (Das christliche Adambuch des Morgenlandes). The second part is from the Greek Revelation of Moses (in Tischendorf's Apocalypses Apocryphae), and from the Latin Life of Adam, edited by W. Meyer.

The first part of the story of Abraham is from The Apocalypse of Abraham, translated from Slavonic by Professor N. Bonwetsch; the second part is from The Testament of Abraham, edited by me in Texts and Studies.

The story of Aseneth is from the Greek History of Aseneth, edited by Batiffol in Studia Patristica.

The story of Job is taken from The Testament of Job in my Apocrypha Anecdota (ii).

That of Solomon is from The Testament of Solomon as printed by Migne at the end of the works of Michael Psellus.

That of Baruch from The Rest of the Words of Baruch, edited by Dr. J. Rendel Harris.

That of Ahikar principally from the French edition by the Abbe F. Nau, with some few touches borrowed from that by Dr. J. Rendel Harris.

One last word. Not all of the stories in this book are equally old. The oldest is most likely that of Ahikar. Lately some pieces of it have been discovered in Egypt in a very ancient copy. Next, probably, comes the second part of the story of Adam. In each of the others there are some parts which are derived from early Jewish tales, but the books in which we have them now were put into their present shape by Christians. Still, there is not one that is less than fifteen hundred years old.

# OLD TESTAMENT LEGENDS

## ADAM

When Adam and Eve were driven out of the Garden of Eden, they were as helpless as little children. They knew nothing of day or night, heat or cold; they could not kindle a fire to warm themselves, nor till the ground to grow food. They had as yet no clothes to wear and no shelter against rain or sun. As long as they were in the garden, it was always light and warm, and their bodies were so fashioned that they had no need of food or sleep or of protection against the burning of the sun; but since they had eaten of the Tree of Knowledge, they had become like us. Moreover, all the beasts and birds were friendly with them; but now they knew that it was not so, and that they had no defence if any fierce animal chose to attack them; and, more than all, they knew that they had a cruel enemy lying in wait for them outside the garden, even Satan, who had hated them from the first, and had brought about their fall by means of the serpent. And so it was that when they came out of the gate of the garden and saw the earth stretched out before them, covered with rocks and sand, and found themselves in a strange land where there was no one to guide them, they fell down on their faces, and became as dead, because of the misery and sorrow which they felt. But God looked upon them and sent His Word to raise them up and comfort them; and showed them a place not very far from the garden where there was a cave; and told them that they were to live there. Now this was the cave which was afterwards called the Cave of Treasures.

When first they entered into the cave, they did nothing but weep and lament: not only because they had lost the garden, but also because for the first time the sky was hidden from them by the roof of the cave; for as yet they had never been in any place where they could not see it. But when the sun set and there was darkness outside the cave as well as inside, they were frightened beyond measure; for they said, "It is because of what we have done: the light is gone out of the heavens, and will come back no more." Then the Word of God spake to them and said, "Be comforted; it is only so for a few hours, and the light will return to you." And they remained praying and weeping in the cave until the darkness began to grow less. After that the sun rose, and Adam went to the mouth of the cave, and it shone full upon him, and he felt the burning heat of it on his body for the first time, and thought that it was God who had come to afflict and punish him; and he beat upon his breast and prayed for mercy. But God said, "This sun is not God; it is created to give light to the world, and every day it will rise in like manner, and travel over the heavens and set, as you have seen it. I am God, who comforted you in the night."

Then Adam and Eve took courage, and came out of the cave, and thought they would go towards the garden; and when they came near to the gate by which they had been driven out of it, they met the serpent. Now before it tempted Eve and became accursed, the serpent had been the most beautiful of all the creatures. Its head was of all the colours of the most beautiful jewels; it had eyes like emeralds, and a melodious voice; it had slender and graceful legs, and it fed on perfumed flowers and delicious fruits. Now it was loathsome to look upon; it wriggled on its belly in the dust, and all creatures spurned and hated it. And when it saw Eve it was enraged to think of the curse that had come upon it through her, and it raised itself up and darted at her, and its eyes became blood-red with anger. Then Adam, who had nothing in his hand wherewith to defend Eve, ran and caught it by the tail, but it turned upon him and coiled about him and Eve with its body and began to crush them; and it said, "It is because of you that I am compelled to trail in the dust and have lost my beauty." And they cried out for fear. But God sent an angel who caught hold of the serpent and loosed them, and smote the serpent with dumbness, so that thereafter it could only hiss. And a great wind came and took it up, and cast it away upon the seashore of India.

And when Adam and Eve had a little recovered themselves from their fear, they went on towards the garden; but at the gate of it there stood a great cherub holding a sword of fire; and when they were able to look upon his face, they saw that he was angry and that he frowned upon them, and raised his sword as if he would smite them with it; but he said nothing. So they were in great fear, and turned from him and went back in great sorrow of heart, wandering they knew not whither, until they found themselves standing on the top of a rock, and before their feet was a precipice. And Adam was so miserable that he desired to live no longer; and he cast himself down from the top of the rock, and lay on the ground below without moving; and Eve thought that he was dead, and said, "I will not live after him; it is through my fault that all these evils have come upon him." And she also threw herself down from the top of the rock; but though both of them were torn and bruised, they were not wounded to death. And after a long time they came to themselves.

Then they bethought them that they had done wrong in trying to put an end to their own lives before it pleased God to set them free from this world. Therefore Adam took stones and piled them up in the shape of an altar, and then they gathered leaves from the trees and wiped off the blood that had been spilt upon the face of the rock, and gathered up the dust that was mingled with their blood and laid it upon the altar, and prayed to God to forgive their trespass. And this was the first offering that they made to God. And God looked upon them with pity and forgave them, and said, "As you have shed your blood, so after five thousand and five hundred years have passed will I take your flesh upon Me and shed My blood for you and for your children; and it shall have power to quench the flame of the sword which is in the hand of the angel, and you shall enter again into the garden, and dwell there until the time when I shall make a new heaven and a new earth."

But when Satan saw that God had pity upon Adam and Eve and accepted their humble offering—for he was all this time keeping watch to see what would become of them—he was filled with dismay and hate, and began to contrive means by which he might lead them astray and put an end to them; for he thought, "If these creatures were destroyed, the earth would remain to me and to my hosts, and I should reign over it alone." He called therefore for some of his host, and made them appear like angels of light. And when they were all disguised in this fashion, they rose into the air and flew towards the cave, from which Adam and Eve were just coming out, meaning to go once again towards the garden. When they caught sight of these bright ones in the air, they stopped and raised their hands towards them, thinking that they were angels coming to them with a message. Satan called to Adam, "Adam, we are angels come from God; He has sent us to bring you to the lake of pure water that is on the north side of Eden, that you may wash yourselves in it and be cleansed from your sin, and return once more to the garden. Come therefore and follow us." And they turned and began flying towards the north; but Adam and Eve were glad beyond measure, and followed the troop of angels as quickly as they could, till they came to the mountain on the north side of Eden which overhung the lake. Then Satan lighted on the ground, and guided them to the top of the mountain, which was very steep. And when they were at the summit, they stood for a while and looked down upon the waters of the lake; and while they were doing so, Satan vanished away silently, and all his host with him; so that when Adam and Eve looked round, they found themselves left alone and in great peril. And they saw that they had been brought into this danger by Satan, and that he had deceived them once again. And they cried aloud for help.

Then God had pity on them, and commanded the angels Sariel and Salathiel to bear them in their arms and carry them back to their cave. And when they were come there, Adam prayed to God that, if they might not be permitted to go into the garden any more, He would at least give them something for a remembrance of it to comfort them. So God commanded the archangel Michael to go as far as the Sea of India, and fetch thence some gold, and dip it in the water that flows from under the Tree of Life, and give it to Adam. Likewise He commanded Gabriel to speak to the cherub that kept the gate of the garden, and go in and fetch some frankincense; and Raphael to bring myrrh also from the garden. And they did so. And Michael brought seventy rods of gold, and Gabriel twelve pounds weight of frankincense, and Raphael three pounds of myrrh; and these were all laid up in the cave where Adam and Eve lived: wherefore it was called the Cave of Treasures. And when the appointed time was fulfilled, and the Word took upon Him the flesh of the sons of Adam, three kings came from the East to do Him honour, and offered to Him that same gold and frankincense and myrrh, which had come down to them through many generations.

After some days, Adam and Eve made a vow that they would go, one of them to the river Tigris and the other to the river Euphrates, and would wade into the water up to the neck, and stand there for forty whole days and nights, praying earnestly that they might be forgiven; for even yet they went on hoping that, if they accomplished some great act of repentance, they might be permitted to return into Eden. They separated, therefore, and stood in the water of the river, fasting and praying. But Satan suspected that they had made such a vow, and it frightened him, for he did not feel sure that God would not change His purpose and forgive them; and he said to himself, "I will take care that they shall not keep their vow." Accordingly, on the thirty-fifth day, as Eve stood praying in the water, she heard a voice as of an angel praising God, and she looked and saw one in bright raiment coming to her, and he called to her and said, "God has forgiven Adam! All is well. I have just now brought the good tidings to Adam, and he bade me come and tell you; and lest you should doubt of the truth, he said, 'Remind her of the sign which was given to us in the cave: how the angels brought the gold and laid it on the south side, and the incense on the east, and the myrrh on the west.'" Then Eve was sure that the messenger spoke true, and she rejoiced greatly, and came, as well as she could, out of the water, and followed him. But when they came in sight of the river Euphrates, she saw Adam still standing in the water praying, and she knew that she had been deceived; and at that moment Satan vanished away, and Eve fell upon the ground, for she was stiff with the cold, and weak with fasting. As for Adam, when he saw her, he cried out and smote upon his breast, and sank down into the water, and would have perished but that God sent His angel and drew him up out of the water. And he showed Adam that he could not by these means gain admittance to the garden before the time appointed was fulfilled.

After these things God showed Adam and Eve the things that were necessary for their life. For as yet they had eaten nothing since they came out of the garden; because the food which they had when they were there was heavenly food, and it sustained them through all these many days. Neither had they any clothes. Therefore God told them to go to the seashore, and there they should find the skins of some sheep whose flesh had been devoured by lions, and these skins they should take and make them into raiment. But Satan heard the words of God, and immediately went to the place where the skins were, with intent to throw them into the sea, or burn them with fire; only, just as he was about to seize them, God spake a word, and Satan was bound there immovable, in his own hideous form. And when Adam and Eve came to the place, they saw him crouching beside the skins; and they were afraid at the horrible look of him. Then the Word came to them, saying, "This is he who promised to make you as gods. What have you gained, think you, by hearkening to his words?" And Satan was cowed, and fled away in shame.

Adam and Eve therefore took the sheep-skins, and there came an angel who showed them how to sew them together with palm-thorns and sinews, and they made them into raiment.

Again, God showed them a land where corn was growing, and told them how they might use it for bread; for it was ripe, and they gathered the ears and made an offering of the first ears. And Satan came and burnt part of the corn; but the angels drove him away.

Many other times also did Satan try to destroy Adam and Eve, coming to them disguised as an angel and enticing them into the wilderness; and again, when they were sleeping on the side of a mountain outside their cave, he loosened a great rock above them that it might fall and crush them; but the angels of God caught it and fixed it like a roof over the heads of Adam and Eve, and when they awoke they were astonished. And once he fell upon Adam and smote him in the side with a sharp stone so that he almost slew him. Nevertheless, in all these perils Adam and Eve put their trust in God, and He protected them and healed them. And after a time Satan perceived that he would not be able to destroy them by injuring their bodies, and that they would not listen to him when he tempted them to disobey God. So Satan's war against Adam was defeated.

This is the first part of the story of Adam, as it is told in an old book called The Conflict of Adam and Eve. It is only part of the story; I have left out a great deal. The second part of the story is taken from a Greek book called The Revelation of Moses, and a Latin one called The Life of Adam and Eve. It tells how Adam died and was buried.

# THE DEATH OF ADAM AND EVE

Adam lived for 930 years; and there were born to him thirty sons and thirty daughters. And when he was 930 years old he fell sick, and sent for all his children, and for their children also, saying, "Come and let me see you before I die." They all gathered together therefore at the door of his dwelling, saving Cain, who was a wanderer upon the face of the earth; but Seth was the eldest of those that came, and he was the most beloved son of Adam and Eve.

And Seth said to his father, "Father, what is the matter with you?" And Adam answered, "Great pain and sickness is upon me." And his children said, "What mean you by pain and sickness?" For as yet no one had died upon the earth except Abel, whom Cain slew. Then said Seth, "Father, is it because you long after the garden and desire the fruit of it? If it be so, command me, and I will go to the gate, and cast dust upon my head, and weep and pray; and God will send His angel, and it may be He will suffer me to bring you some of the fruit of the garden, and you shall eat it and recover." Eve also wept and said, "My lord Adam, give me the half of your disease, and let me bear it for you; because it is through my fault that this evil has come upon you." Then said Adam, "I will tell you what you shall do, even you and my son Seth: you shall go to the garden and pray there as you have said, and ask the angel to give me some of the oil of mercy that flows from the Tree of Life, and bring it to me that I may anoint my body with it, and be eased from my pain."

So Eve and Seth departed and went towards the garden; and as they were going through the woods, a wild beast leaped out and attacked Seth. And Eve was terrified and cried out, "Alas! alas! what will become of me at the last day? Surely all that have done evil will curse me, saying, 'Woe unto Eve, because she kept not the commandment of God!'" And she cried out upon the wild beast, "How wast thou not afraid to fight against the image of God? How is thy mouth opened against Him? Dost thou not remember that God put thee in subjection to us?" And the beast spake with a man's voice and said, "What have we to do with thy weeping and complaints? How was it that thy mouth was opened to eat of the fruit? Accuse me not, lest I begin to accuse thee." Then said Seth to the beast, "Shut thy mouth: be silent: dare not to touch the image of

God." And the beast answered, "Thee will I obey, O Seth." And it fled and left him wounded, and went back to its den.

So Eve and Seth went on to the garden and wept before the gate, beseeching God to send them the oil of mercy for Adam. And God sent Michael the archangel to them, who said, "Seth, thou man of God, weary not thyself with making supplication for the oil of mercy, for it cannot be given to thee now. But when the times are fulfilled, then shall come One who shall anoint thy father with that oil, and he shall rise up and return to the garden, he and all his seed; and the evil heart shall be taken from them, and a new heart shall be given them to understand that which is good, and God shall dwell in the midst of them, and they shall be His people. But now go back to thy father, for his end is near, even within three days, and tell him these words; and watch what shall come to pass when he is taken from thee." They returned therefore to Adam, and told him; and he groaned and said, "Alas! O Eve, what is this that thou hast done, to bring upon us the dominion of death? Now therefore call together our children and our children's children, and tell them concerning our sin, from first to last." So, when they were assembled, Eve spoke to them, and told them the whole story of how Satan came to the serpent and taunted it for paying homage to Adam and Eve, forasmuch as they were neither so beautiful nor so wise as itself; and he persuaded the serpent to let him speak through its mouth; and at the hour when the angels go up to the heavens to worship God, the serpent slipped over the wall and found Eve by the Tree of Knowledge; and of what happened after that, until the time when they were cast out of the garden. And when she ceased speaking, her children departed.

Then she went in to Adam, and said to him,

"How can I live when you are dead? and how long will it be before I also die? Tell me." Adam answered, "Trouble not yourself; for you will not tarry long after me, and I believe that the same grave will hold both of us. But now, when I die, leave me alone, and let no one touch me until the will of God is made known concerning me. For I am sure that God will not forget me, but will visit the creature which His hands have made. Now therefore go and pray to Him until I give up my spirit to Him that gave it; for we know not how we shall meet Him, whether He will yet be wroth with us, or whether He will turn and have mercy upon us." She went out therefore and fell upon the ground and prayed a long time.

And at last the Angel of Mankind came to her and said, "Rise up,

Eve; for Adam thy husband is departing out of this life, and is going to meet Him that made him."

Eve therefore arose and looked up into the sky; and she saw a chariot of light coming, drawn by four shining eagles, and angels on either side escorting the chariot. And when it came above the place where our father Adam lay, it stayed. And the angels came bearing censers, and they stood about it and lighted their censers, and the smoke of the incense rose up and hid the firmament; and the angels bowed and worshipped, saying, "Holy One, have mercy, for he is Thine image and the work of Thy hands."

Also Eve beheld two great and fearful ones standing in the heavens, and she was afraid and called upon Seth, saying, "Rise up, O Seth, and come to me, and behold that which no eye of man hath looked upon." So he came to her, and she said, "Seest thou the seven heavens open, and thy father Adam lying upon his face and the holy angels interceding for him?" She said, moreover, "Who are the two dark ones that stand praying for thy father?" And Seth answered, "They are the Sun and the Moon, who are entreating the Most High for my father Adam." And Eve said, "Where then is their light, and why is their aspect black?" And he said, "They cannot shine in the presence of the Light of all things: therefore is their light departed from them."

Now as Seth was speaking to his mother, behold, the angels blew with the trumpets, and fell on their faces, and cried with a loud voice, "Blessed be the glory of the Lord over all His works; for He hath had compassion upon Adam, the work of His hands." Then came one of the Seraphim, having six wings, and caught up the soul of Adam and bare it to the lake of pure water which is on the north side of Eden, and washed it before the face of God. And the Most High commanded him to deliver it unto Michael the archangel, that he should bear it into Paradise until the day of the visitation of all things.

After that the holy archangel entreated the Most High concerning the body of Adam. And God commanded all the angels to come before Him, every one in his order; and they gathered themselves together, bearing censers and trumpets and vials full of odours. And the Lord of Hosts went up, and the great winds before Him, and the Cherubim flying upon the winds, and the angels of heaven round about Him. And they bore up the body of Adam and carried it into the garden. And all the trees of the garden bowed and swayed and gave forth their odours. And because of the greatness of that sight, and of the sweetness of the odours of Paradise, all the sons of Adam, and all that were on the earth, were cast into a deep sleep, saving Seth only.

Now as the body of Adam lay in Paradise, God said, "O Adam, why didst thou transgress My commandment? For if thou hadst kept it, they that persecute thee would not have rejoiced against thee. Nevertheless I say unto thee, that hereafter I will turn their joy into sorrow, and thy sorrow into joy."

Then the angels brought shrouds of silk and fine linen, and God commanded Michael, Gabriel, Uriel, and Raphael, and they wrapped up the body of Adam therein, and anointed it with sweet odours. And the Lord said, "Bring hither also the body of Abel." For since the day when Cain slew him, the body of Abel had not been buried: because Cain often sought to hide it, but the earth would not receive it, until the dust that was first taken out of her and made into a body, that is, the body of Adam, should be restored to her.

So the body of Abel was brought and wrapped in grave-clothes like that of Adam; and they were both of them buried in the place from which God took the dust when He formed Adam at the first, and the angels dug the grave and covered it in.

And when this was done, God called to the body, saying, "Adam, Adam!" And the body answered, "Here am I, Lord." And the Lord said, "I said unto thee, 'Dust thou art and unto dust shalt thou return.' Behold now I promise thee that in the last days I will raise thee up yet again out of the dust, even thee and all thy seed with thee." And God sealed the tomb that no man should touch it until six days were fulfilled, and the rib which was taken out of Adam should be given back to him.

After these things Eve awoke out of her sleep, and was troubled because she knew not what had become of the body of Adam; and she prayed, saying, "Lord, as Thou didst make me out of the flesh of Adam, and as I was with him in the garden, and after we were cast out I was never parted from him, so now, I beseech thee, suffer me to be buried with him, and let no man part us asunder." And on the seventh day after the death of Adam, Eve was thus praying; and when she had ended her prayer, she looked up into heaven and smote her breast and said, "Lord God of all things, receive my spirit." And so she gave up her soul to God.

And immediately the angels came and took her body, and buried it in the place where the bodies of Adam and Abel were laid.

# ABRAHAM

Abraham was the son of Terah, and Terah was a maker of idols which he sold to the people round about him. Now this is the story of how Abraham came to believe in the true God; and in the ancient book the story is put into the mouth of Abraham himself, and he tells it in this way:

I was troubled in my mind because I desired to know who was in truth the strongest of all the Gods. And one day when I was attending to the gods of my father Terah, gods of wood and stone, gold and silver, iron and brass, I went into the temple where they stood, and found that one of them, the god named Marumath, who was carved out of stone, had fallen over and was lying at the feet of the god Zucheus. When I saw that, I was alarmed, and thought that I should never be able to put him back in his place by myself, because he was so heavy; so I went and told my father, and he came, and the two of us could hardly manage to move him; but as we were doing so, the head of the god broke off in my hands. At that my father said, "Abraham", and I said, "Here am I, bring me the chisels out of the house." And when I had done so, he fashioned another Marumath out of stone, without a head, and fixed the head that had come off the first Marumath upon it; and the rest of the old Marumath he broke in pieces.

After that he made five more gods, and bade me take them and sell them in the streets of the city; and I saddled the ass, and put them upon it, and went to the river to sell them; and there I found merchants coming from Fandana in Syria with camels, on their way to Egypt to bring papyrus from the Nile. And as I was talking with them one of their camels belched, and the donkey took fright and ran off, and the gods fell off its back, and three of them were broken, and only two remained whole. But when the Syrians saw what had happened, they said, "Why did you not tell us that you had gods to sell? We might have bought them before the donkey took fright, and they would not have been destroyed; at least we will take the gods that remain, and pay you the price of them all." And they did so; and the broken gods I cast into the river Gur, and they sank and were seen no more.

But as I returned home, I was bewildered and divided in my mind. I said to myself, "What an evil trade is this that my father practises! Is not he in truth the god of his own gods which he makes with his chisels and lathes and his skill? Ought they not rather to worship him than he them? Surely it is all deceit. Look at Marumath, who fell and could not get up again, and these five other gods which could not punish the donkey for running away with them, nor keep themselves from being broken and thrown into the river."

And as I was thinking of all these things, I arrived at my father's house. Then I gave the ass his hay and water, and went in and gave the price of the gods to my father Terah, and he was pleased and said, "Blessed be thou of my gods: my labour has not been in vain." But I said, "It is rather thou, father, that givest blessing to the gods, for thou art their god; their own blessing is vain and their help is naught: if they cannot help themselves, how should they help thee or bless me?" But he was very angry with me for speaking lightly of his gods.

Then I went out of the house, and after a while my father called me and said, "Gather up the chips of the fig-wood wherewith I was making gods before you came in, and see about preparing dinner."

And as I was doing so, I found a little god lying among the straw and the rubbish, and on his forehead was written: "The god Barisat." So I kept him, and did not tell my father; and when I had kindled the fire to cook the dinner, and was going out to fetch the food, I set Barisat down in front of the fire and said to him, "Barisat, take care that the fire does not go out before I come back; and if it does, blow upon it and revive it." Then I went out and did my errand, and when I returned I found Barisat fallen over backwards, and his feet were in the fire and were badly burnt; and I laughed to myself and said, "You are in truth a good fireman and cook, Barisat." Just then the fire caught upon his body and burnt him all up.

When the time was come, I brought food to my father and he ate, and I gave him wine and milk and he drank, and rejoiced and praised his god Marumath; and I said, "Father, you should not praise Marumath, but rather Barisat, for he has done more for you: he has thrown himself into the fire to cook your dinner." "And where is he now?" said my father. "He has been burnt to ashes," I said, "in the heat of the fire, and nothing but dust is left of him." And my father said, "Great is the strength of Barisat! I will make another one to-day, and he shall prepare my food for me to-morrow." Now when I heard my father say these words, I laughed in myself, and yet I was troubled and angry in my soul. And at last I answered and said, "Whichever of these things you honour as a god, it is folly. The god Zucheus, who is the god of my brother Nahor, is more honourable than your god Marumath, for he is adorned with gold finely wrought, and when he is old he will be fashioned over again; but if Marumath is broken or injured he will not be renewed, for he is only of stone. And again the god Joauv, who stands next to Zucheus, is more honourable than Barisat, for he is covered with silver; but as for Barisat, you made him yourself with your axe, and, look, he is fallen upon the earth, and the fashion of his likeness is destroyed, and he is burnt to ashes, and you say, 'To-day I will make another, and he shall prepare my food to-morrow.'

"But I say to you, my father, the fire is mightier than all your gods of gold and silver and stone and wood, for it can devour them all. Yet I call not the fire god, for it is weaker than the water which can subdue it. Yet again I call not the water god, for the earth swallows it up. Neither call I the earth god, for it is subject to men that till it, and to the sun that gives light to it. Neither call I the sun god, for it is overcome by the darkness of night. But I say that there is one true God who hath made all these things; who hath made the heavens blue, and the sun golden, and the moon and stars white and shining, and hath raised up the earth from among the waters, and breathed into thee the breath of life, and hath sought me out in the trouble of my soul; and would that He might reveal Himself unto us!"

And as I was speaking these words to my father in the court of his house, there came from heaven the voice of a Mighty One speaking out of a cloud of fire, and said, "Abraham, Abraham!" And I said, "Behold, here am I!" And He said, "In the thought of thy heart thou seekest after the God of Gods and the Maker of all things: I am He. Depart from thy father Terah and go out of his house, lest thou be consumed in his wickedness." And I went out; and it came to pass, as I came to the door of the house, that there fell a noise of a great thundering, and the fire fell and burnt up my father Terah and his house and all that was therein.

This is the story of the beginning of the life of Abraham; and that which is told about the end of his life is as follows:

Abraham had lived out the measure of his days. He was now a hundred and seventy-five years old, and all the days of his life he had lived in kindness and meekness and uprightness: and especially was he hospitable and courteous to strangers. He dwelt by the cross-roads near the oak of Mamre, and entertained all the wayfarers who came that way, rich and poor, lame and sound, friends or strangers.

But at last to him, as to all other men, there came the bitter cup of death, which none can put away. So when the time was come, the Most High called to him the archangel Michael and said to him, "Michael, prince of the host, go down to Abraham and speak to him concerning his death, that he may set his house in order: for his possessions are great. Announce to him therefore that he is to depart speedily out of the earthly life, and come to his Lord in peace and happiness."

Michael therefore went forth from the presence of the Lord and went down to Abraham at the oak of Mamre, and found him in the fields hard by, watching his husbandmen ploughing with their oxen. And Abraham lifted up his eyes and saw Michael coming towards him in the dress and fashion of a soldier—for he was the captain of the Lord's host—very beautiful to look upon. And Abraham rose and went to meet him, as was his custom with all strangers; and when they had saluted one another, Abraham asked Michael whence he came; and Michael answered, "I come from the Great City, and my errand is to fetch a certain friend of the Great King, whom He is inviting to come to Him." Then said Abraham, "My lord, come with me to my house." And when Michael consented, Abraham called one of his men and bade him fetch two quiet horses that he and the stranger might ride home on them. But Michael refused, for he knew that no earthly horse could bear him; so he said, "Nay, but rather let us go on foot to your house."

And as they went up from the fields, they came to a cypress-tree growing by the wayside; and as they passed by it there came from it a human voice, which said, "Holy is the Lord who calleth to Himself them that love Him." Now this happened by the commandment of God, to be a sign to Abraham, and he marvelled; but when he looked at his companion and saw that he seemed to take no notice of it, he said nothing, thinking that only he had heard the voice. Soon after they came to the house, and Isaac and Sarah came to greet them, and they sat down in the courtyard of the house. But Isaac said to his mother Sarah, "Mother, I am sure that the man who is sitting with my father is not of the race of men that live on the earth." Just then Abraham called to Isaac, "Isaac, my son, draw water from the well, and bring it to me in a basin, that we may wash the stranger's feet, for he has come a long journey." So Isaac ran and fetched the water to his father; and Abraham said to him secretly, "My child, something says to me that this will be the last time that I shall wash the feet of any stranger coming to this house." And Isaac was greatly distressed and said, "What mean you, father, by these words?" Abraham said nothing, but stooped down and began to wash the feet of Michael; and Isaac wept. Abraham too shed tears, and Michael seeing it, was moved with pity, and wept also; and his tears fell into the basin of water and became precious pearls. When Abraham saw that, he marvelled; but he gathered up the pearls secretly and said nothing.

After that he told Isaac to go and prepare the banqueting-room, spread two couches, light the lamps, burn sweet odours, and fetch fragrant herbs and flowers from the garden. "For," said he, "this man who is come to us is worthy of all the honour we can do him." So Isaac went to make ready the room, and Sarah also set about preparing a feast. Then, while they were all busying themselves with preparation, the sun began to set, and the hour came at which all the angels appear before God and worship Him; and Michael also flew up into the heavens in the twinkling of an eye, and stood before the Lord. And when all the angels had done their worship and gone forth again, Michael remained and said to the Lord, "Lord, I cannot speak to Abraham about his death; for I have never seen his like upon the earth, kind, courteous, hospitable, fearing God, and keeping himself pure from all evil. I cannot grieve his heart by telling him that he is to die." And the Lord said, "Go down again to my friend Abraham, and whatsoever he would have thee do, do it; and I will put the thought of his death into the mind of his son Isaac in a dream. Then Isaac shall tell the dream, and thou shalt interpret it, and so Abraham shall be certified of his death."

So Michael returned to Abraham's house, and sat at meat with him, and Isaac waited on them; and after supper, Abraham offered up prayer as he was wont, and the archangel prayed with him, and they went to their beds. Isaac also asked his father if he might sleep with them, for he desired exceedingly to be near the wonderful stranger and to hear his words; but Abraham said, "Nay, my son, lest we be burdensome to the stranger." Therefore Isaac bowed down and received his father's blessing, and went to his own chamber.

And about the third hour of the night Isaac dreamed a dream, and it frightened him, so that he leapt out of bed and ran hastily to the room where Abraham and Michael were sleeping, and beat upon the door and said, "Father, open to me quickly! let me kiss you once again before they take you away from me." Then Abraham opened the door, and Isaac ran in and hung upon his neck, weeping loudly. And Sarah was awakened by the noise of the weeping, and came quickly to them; and she also wept and said, "What is the matter?

Has our brother who is come to us brought you evil tidings of Lot, your nephew?" But Michael said, "No, lady, it is not so; but, as I think, your son Isaac has dreamed a dream which has troubled him, so he came to us weeping, and we were moved at the sight of his tears, and wept with him."

Now Sarah, when she heard the sound of the voice of Michael, became sure in her own mind that it was an angel of God who was speaking. She beckoned therefore to Abraham to come to her at the door of the house, and took him aside and said to him, "Do you know who this man is?" and he said, "No." "Do you remember," said she, "the three men who came to us once at the oak of Mamre; and how you killed a calf and prepared a feast for them; and how when the calf was eaten, it suddenly became whole again and sprang up and ran and suckled its mother? I am sure that this is one of those three men." Abraham answered, "Sarah, you have hit the truth; praised be God for His wonders. Now I tell you that last night when I was washing the feet of this man, I said to myself, 'Surely these are the feet that I washed long ago under the oak-tree?' And furthermore, he shed tears, and they fell into the water and became these pearls." And he drew the pearls out of his bosom and showed them to her, and she bowed her head and praised God and said, "Be sure, Abraham, that he is come to reveal some matter to us, whether for evil or for good."

Then Abraham left Sarah and went in and said to Isaac, "Come here, my child, and tell me what you saw, and what caused you to come to us in such haste?" And Isaac said, "It was this, father. I saw in a dream this night the sun and the moon upon my head, and the rays of the sun were all about me and enlightened me, and I rejoiced in them; then I saw the heavens opening, and a shining man, brighter than seven suns, came down; and he approached me and took the sun from off my head and carried it up into heaven; and again after a little while, as I was sorrowing over it, he came and took the moon from me. Then I was greatly distressed, and I besought him, saying, 'Nay, my lord, do not take all my glory from me; have pity upon me; if thou must needs take the sun, yet leave me the moon.' But he said, 'Suffer them to be taken up to the King above, for He desires them to be with Him.' So he took them away, saying, 'They are removed from toil unto rest, and from darkness unto light.' But their glory he left upon me. Then I awoke." And Isaac ceased speaking.

Then Michael said, "Hear me, righteous Abraham. The sun which Isaac saw is you, his father; the moon likewise is Sarah, his mother;

and the shining one who came down out of heaven and took them away is myself. And now be it known to you that the time is come for you to leave this earthly life and go to God." But Abraham said, "Why, here is a marvel indeed! And are you the one appointed to take my soul from me?" He answered, "I am Michael, the captain of the host of God, and I am sent to speak to you concerning your death." Then said Abraham, "I know that you are an angel of God, and that you are sent to take away my soul. But I shall not follow you!"

When Michael heard that word he vanished away from them and went up to the heavens and stood before the Lord, and told Him what Abraham had said; and the Lord answered, "Return to Abraham My friend and speak yet again to him, Thus saith the Lord: 'I brought thee out of thy father's house into the land of promise: I have blessed thee and increased thee more than the sands of the seashore and more than the stars of heaven. Why dost thou resist My decree? Knowest thou not that Adam and Eve died, and all their offspring; none of the forefathers escaped death; they are all of them gone unto the place of spirits, all of them have been gathered by the sickle of death. And I have not suffered the angel of death to approach thee: I have not permitted any evil disease to come upon thee, but instead I have sent mine own prince Michael to speak peaceably unto thee, that thou mayest set thine house in order and bless thy son Isaac and depart in peace; and now thou sayest, "I will in nowise follow him." Knowest thou not that if I send Death unto thee, thou must needs come whether thou wilt or no?'" So Michael returned to Abraham, and found him weeping, and told him all these words; and Abraham besought him, saying, "Speak yet once again to my Lord and say to Him, 'Thus saith Abraham Thy servant: Lord, Thou hast been gracious to me all my life long, and now, behold, I do not resist Thy word, for I know that I am a mortal man; but this one thing I ask of Thee, that while I am yet in my body Thou wouldst suffer me to see Thy world and all the creatures that Thou hast made. Then shall I depart out of this life without any trouble of mind.'" And Michael returned and spake all these words before the Lord, and the Lord said, "Take a cloud of light and angels that have power over the chariots, and bear Abraham in the chariot of the cherubim into the air of heaven and let him see all the world before he dies."

And it was done; and Michael showed Abraham all the regions of the world. He saw men ploughing and carting, keeping flocks, dancing, sporting, and playing the harp, wrestling, going to law, weeping, dying, and being carried out to burial: even all the things that are done in the earth, both good and evil. And in one place they saw men with swords in their hands, and Abraham asked Michael, "Who are these?" And Michael said, "These are thieves who are going out to steal and to kill and to destroy." Then Abraham said, "O that God would hear me and send evil beasts out of the forest to devour them!" And in that moment wild beasts rushed out upon them and tore them to pieces. Then in another place he saw men and women feasting and drinking before their idols, and he said, "O that the earth might open and swallow them up!" And immediately it happened as he had said. And in yet another place he saw men breaking through the wall of a house to enter it and rob it; and he prayed again, and fire fell from heaven and burnt them up. Then there came a voice which said, "Michael, prince of My host, turn the chariot and bring Abraham back, lest, if he sees any more of the sinners upon earth, he destroy the whole race of men. For he is a righteous man, and has no compassion upon sinners. But I created the world, and I would not have any perish. Bring Abraham therefore to the entering in of the gate of heaven, that he may see the judgment and the recompensing of men, and may have pity upon the souls whom he has blotted out."

Michael therefore turned the chariot and brought Abraham across the great river of Ocean to the entering in of the gate of heaven, and showed him the judgments. And Abraham saw the narrow gate of life and the broad gate of destruction, and between the gates he saw our father Adam sitting upon a throne, and clad in a glorious robe of many colours; and he saw how Adam lamented when the souls went in through the broad gate, and how he rejoiced when they attained to the narrow gate, and how his weeping exceeded his rejoicing. Moreover, Michael showed him how the souls of men are examined concerning their works and how their acts are re-corded and weighed. But when he saw how hard it is to enter in at the strait gate, it repented him that he had prayed for the punishment of the sinners, and he said to Michael, "O prince of the host, let us entreat the Lord that He would have mercy upon the souls of the men whom I cursed in my anger; for now I know that I sinned before God when I prayed against them." Then they both prayed earnestly to God; and after a long time there came a voice saying, "Abraham, I have heard thy prayer, and I have given back life to the men whom thou didst destroy."

Moreover, the voice bade Michael take Abraham back to his house. And when he was come thither, he went up to the great chamber, and sat upon the couch; and Sarah and Isaac came and fell on his neck, and all his servants gathered about him, rejoicing at his return. And Michael said, "Hearken, Abraham: here is Sarah your wife and Isaac your son, and here are all your manservants and maidservants about you. Now therefore set in order your house and bless them, and make ready to depart with me, for your hour is come." Abraham answered, "Did the Lord command you to say this, or do you say it of yourself?" Michael said, "The Lord commanded me, and I give the message to you." Yet for all that Abraham answered, "I will not follow you." So Michael went forth and stood before the Most High again and told him the words of Abraham; and he said besides, "I cannot lay hands upon him, for there is not his like upon the earth, no, not even the righteous Job. Tell me therefore, Lord, what I must do."

And God said, "Call Death, and bid him come hither." Michael went and found Death, and said to him, "Come, for the Lord of all things, the Immortal King, calleth for thee." And Death trembled and feared exceedingly when he heard that; but he followed Michael and came and stood before the Lord, quivering and shaking with fear, awaiting the commands of his Master. And God said to him, "Hide thy hideous appearance, cover up thy corruption, put away from thee all thy terror, and put on a glorious and beautiful aspect, and go down to Abraham My friend and take him and bring him to Me: only see that thou make him not afraid, but bring him peaceably, for he is My friend." So Death went forth from the presence of God, and made himself like an angel of light, beautiful to look upon, and departed to seek Abraham. Now Abraham had come down from his chamber and was sitting under the trees of Mamre, leaning his head upon his hand, expecting the return of Michael the archangel. And suddenly he was aware of a sweet perfume, and of a light shining near him; and he turned round and saw Death coming towards him in a form of great glory and beauty, and rose to meet him, supposing him to be an angel of God. And they greeted one another, and Abraham said, "Whence come you to me, and who are you?" Death answered, "Abraham, I tell you the truth: I am the bitter cup of death." Abraham said, "Rather you are the beauty of the world; a fairer than you I have never seen, and how say you, 'I am the bitter cup of death'?" He answered, "I have told you the truth; the name by which God named me is that which I have spoken." Abraham said, "And why have you come to this place?" Death answered, "I am come to take your soul, O righteous one." Abraham said, "I hear what you say, but I shall not come with you." But Death was silent and answered him not a word.

Then Abraham rose up and went towards his house: and Death followed him. And he went up into his chamber: and Death went with him; and he laid himself on his bed: and Death came and sat by his feet. And Abraham said, "Go, depart from me: I wish to rest here on my couch." Death answered, "I shall not depart till I have taken thy soul from thy body." Abraham said, "I adjure thee by the living God: art thou in very truth Death?" He said, "I am." Then said Abraham, "Comest thou to all men in such a beautiful shape as this?" He said, "Nay, my lord Abraham; it is thy righteousness and thy good deeds which make as it were a crown of glory upon my head; it is only to such as thou art that I come thus peaceably, but to sinners I show myself much otherwise." "Show me then," said Abraham, "in what form thou comest to them: let me see all thy fierceness and bitterness." "No," said Death, "for thou couldst not bear to look upon it." "Verily, I am able to bear it," he said, "for the strength of the God of heaven is with me."

Then Death let fall from him all his beauty, and Abraham saw him as he was. And where there had been a shining angel, he saw a cloud of darkness, and in it the shapes of horrible wild beasts and all unclean creatures; and he saw the heads of fiery dragons, and flames of consuming fire darting out; and he seemed to see a dreadful precipice before him, and then a rushing river, and flashes of lightning, and crackling of thunder, and thereafter a tempestuous raging sea; and again weapons brandished, and venomous basilisks and serpents, and bowls of poison; and there came a horrible odour, so that all the servants of Abraham that were in the chamber fainted and died, and Abraham himself swooned and his senses left him.

When he came to himself, Death had hidden his terrible aspect and put on his beautiful form again. And Abraham saw his servants lying dead, and said to Death, "How is it that thou hast slain these?" And Death said, "They died at the sight of my countenance, and in truth it is a marvel that thou also didst not die with them." "Yea," said Abraham, "now I know how it was that I came by this faintness of spirit that is upon me; but I pray thee, Death, inasmuch as these have been cut off before their time, let us entreat God that he would raise them up again." So Abraham and Death prayed together; and the spirit of life returned into the servants that had been killed, and they rose up again. After that Abraham conversed with Death.

Then Sarah and Isaac came in and talked with Abraham as he lay on his bed. And Abraham said to Death, "I beseech thee, depart from me for a little, for since I looked upon thee weakness is come upon me, and my breath labours and my heart is troubled." Then said Death, "Kiss my right hand and thy strength will return to thee, and thou wilt be filled with joy." So Abraham kissed the hand of Death, and the soul of Abraham clave to the hand of Death and left his body; and straightway Michael was there and a multitude of angels with him, and they accompanied the holy soul of Abraham and brought it into the heavens into the presence of the Most High, there to abide everlastingly in gladness and brightness in the place from which all sorrow and sighing are fled away.

# THE STORY OF ASENETH, JOSEPH'S WIFE

## I

There was once a great man named Potipherah, who was high priest of the city of On in Egypt; and he and his wife had no children. One day he went into the temple to offer sacrifice, as was his custom. He went alone, and when he entered the great courtyard of the temple, in the middle of which stood the altar, he was astonished to see a little child lying upon the altar. Without waiting to offer his sacrifice, he hurried back to his wife. "What is the matter," said she, "that you come back so hastily?" "I have seen a wonderful thing," he said; "the gods have given us a child. The gates of the temple were locked, so that no one could get into the court; yet there is a child there, lying on the altar!" "What say you?" said his wife; "what can be the meaning of it?" So they both hastened to the temple, and when Potipherah opened the door of the courtyard, they saw, partly at least, how the wonder had happened; for now there was an eagle perched upon the altar with its wings spread out over the child—it was a little girl, quite newly born—to protect it. They guessed that it was the eagle that had brought the child, but, of course, they could not tell whose it was. It was wrapped in swaddling-clothes, and these Potipherah's wife kept carefully by her; for she thought the time might come when they might be recognised by the parents of the little child; and indeed, years afterwards, this proved to be the case.

In the meantime Potipherah and his wife kept the child and brought her up, and treated her as their daughter; and they called her Aseneth.

She grew up to be very beautiful; she was quite unlike an Egyptian girl, and might have been taken for a Hebrew maiden: tall as Sarah and lovely as Rebekah or Rachel; so beautiful, in fact, that all the sons of the princes and nobles of Egypt were in love with her, and even the son of King Pharaoh himself said to his father, "Give me Aseneth, the daughter of Potipherah, to wife." But Pharaoh said, "Nay, my son, she is not of your rank; you must marry a queen; remember, the daughter of the King of Moab is affianced to you."

But besides being very beautiful, Aseneth was exceedingly proud. There was not a man of all the young nobles whom she would hear of, much less look at. Indeed, hardly any man in Egypt except her own father had ever seen her face; for she lived apart with the maidens who waited on her, in a lofty tower which her father had built specially for her. It was really a noble palace, with ten great rooms, one over the other. The first room was paved with porphyry and lined with slabs of coloured marbles, and the roof was of gold: and it was a kind of chapel for Aseneth. It had golden and silver images of all the gods of Egypt, and Aseneth worshipped them and burnt incense to them every day. The second chamber was Aseneth's own. In it were all her jewels and rich robes and fine linen. In the third were stored the provisions of the house and every delicious fruit or sweetmeat that could be got from any part of the world. The other seven chambers belonged to the seven maidens who lived with Aseneth and tended her. They were all of one age, and as fair as the stars of heaven, and Aseneth loved them dearly.

But to come back to Aseneth's own chamber, which was the most splendid of all. It had three windows, one looking out upon the garden of the tower towards the east, and another towards the south, and the third towards the high-road. Opposite the eastern window stood a golden bed, with a coverlet woven of gold and purple and fine linen.

And no one but Aseneth herself had ever even sat upon that bed, so magnificent and so sacred was it.

Besides all this, the tower had all around it a garden with a high wall of squared blocks of stone. The gates (there were four of them) were of iron, and each was guarded by eighteen stalwart men in armour. The garden itself was full of shady trees, bearing splendid fruit; and there was a springing fountain at one side of it, whose water ran first into a marble trough, and then out of that into a stream which watered all the garden and kept it fresh and green.

Here Aseneth lived until she was eighteen years old, beautiful and proud and caring for no one except her father and mother and her seven maidens. Now the year in which she became eighteen was the first of the seven years of plenty, of which King Pharaoh had dreamt in the dream of the seven cows and the seven ears of corn, which is written in the Bible. And Joseph was now travelling over all the land of Egypt to gather together corn to store up against the seven years of famine which were to follow the seven of plenty. And upon a certain day in harvest-time, Potipherah and his wife, who had been away at an estate which they possessed in the country, returned to the city of On; and no sooner had they done so than they received a message from Joseph, saying, "Let me come and rest at your house during the heat of the day." Whereupon Potipherah was greatly rejoiced, and thanked the gods for the honour which Joseph did him by visiting him, and ordered a great banquet to be prepared.

Just at this time, Aseneth, who had heard that her father and mother were returned, came to meet them. She had put on her most beautiful robe, of linen woven with gold, and a golden girdle, and necklace and bracelets of precious stones upon which were engraved the names of the gods of Egypt. And she had a golden diadem on her head, and over it a delicate veil. She hastened to meet her father and mother, and they rejoiced at her wonderful beauty, and made her sit by them, and showed her the gifts they had brought to her from the country—grapes and figs, pomegranates and fresh dates, and young doves and quails for her to tame, to her great delight. Then her father said to her, "My child, sit here with us: I want to speak to you." So she sat down between her father and mother, and her father took her hand and kissed her, and said, "My darling child, do you know that Joseph, the lord of all this land, the man who is going to save the country from the famine that is coming the man whom Pharaoh trusts and honours above all others, is coming to this house to-day? What would you say if I were to offer to give you in marriage to him, to live happily with him for the rest of your life?"

Then Aseneth was very angry; she blushed as red as fire, and darted an ugly glance at her father sideways, and said, "How can you talk to me so, father? Would you give me to a creature like that, the son of a Canaanitish labourer, who has been in prison—yes, and sold as a slave—and only got out of prison because he contrived to explain a dream of Pharaoh's, for all the world like the old women? Certainly not! If I marry any one it will be Pharaoh's eldest son." So Potipherah, disappointed as he was, said no more; and Aseneth hurried away to her own chamber. But she looked out of the window.

As she went out, there ran in a young man, one of Potipherah's servants, and said, "My lord, Joseph is just stopping before our gates." So Potipherah and his wife and all their retinue rose and went forth to meet Joseph; and the gates of the court towards the east were thrown open, and the chariot drove in, drawn by four milk-white horses with harness of gold; and in the chariot stood

Joseph, clad in a tunic of white linen and a blood-red mantle shot with gold. On his head was a crown with twelve great gems, and above each gem was a ray of gold; in his hand was an olive branch with leaves and fruit. But fairer than all his equipment was his face, for he was more beautiful than any of the sons of men. And just as all the young nobles of Egypt were mad about Aseneth, so all the ladies of Egypt were in love with Joseph; but he had not a word to say to any of them, for they were all worshippers of idols, and Joseph worshipped the true God—the God of Abraham, Isaac, and Jacob.

So the chariot entered the courtyard of Poti-pherah's palace, and the gates were shut. Now Aseneth stood at her window, and when she saw Joseph and the beauty of his countenance, she was smitten to the heart, her knees trembled, and she almost swooned. A great fear came upon her, and she heaved a deep sigh and said, "Alas, alas, what have I said? what have I done? Pity me, O God of Joseph, for it was in ignorance that I spoke against him. Did I not call him a Canaanitish labourer's son? and lo, now he has come into our house like the sun out of heaven. Fool that I was to rail against him as I did! If only my father would give me to him as his slave and drudge, I would serve him till I dropped dead at his feet."

Meanwhile Joseph, who had caught sight of Aseneth standing at her window, had come into the house, and they had washed his feet and set a table for him by himself (for Joseph would not eat with the Egyptians). And he said to Potipherah, "Who was the woman whom I saw looking out of the window when I came in? Some stranger? If so, she must leave this house." "Nay, my lord," said Potipherah, "she is our daughter." And he went on to tell how Aseneth disliked the company of men, and indeed had hardly seen a strange man before that day; and Joseph was glad to hear that she hated strange men, and said, "If she be your daughter, I will love her from this day forth as a sister."

Accordingly, Aseneth's mother went and fetched Aseneth, and she greeted Joseph, and he her. Then said Potipherah, "Come near, my child, and kiss your brother." But when she drew near, Joseph put out his hand and thrust her away, and spoke thus: "It is not right for one who worships the living God, and eats the bread of life and drinks the cup of immortality, to kiss one that praises with her lips dead idols, and eats the bread of death from their tables and drinks the cup of deceit." At these harsh words Aseneth was bitterly grieved: she shrank back and looked piteously at Joseph, and her eyes filled with tears; and when he saw how hurt she was, Joseph, who was full of kindness raised his hand over her head and blessed her, praying that God, who gives life to all and brings us out of darkness into light, might give life and light to her soul, and number her among His chosen people, and bring her into the everlasting rest which He has promised to them. So Aseneth went back to her chamber, full of mingled joy and sorrow; and she cast herself down on her bed and wept. And that same evening Joseph left the house of Potipherah and set forth on his journey again. "But," said he, "I will come back to you in eight days' time." Potipherah also and his wife and their servants went back to their country house; and Aseneth and her seven maidens were left alone. And the sun went down and all was quiet.

## II

When everyone else in the tower was asleep, Aseneth, who had remained weeping on her bed, rose up stealthily and crept downstairs to the gate of the tower, where the woman who kept the door was asleep with her children; and as quietly as she could she unhooked the heavy leather curtain that hung in the doorway, and spreading it out on the floor, heaped up upon it all the cinders and ashes out of the hearth, folded the corners together, dragged it upstairs and threw it down on the floor. Then she barred the door of her room securely, and burst into bitter weeping. It so happened that the maiden whom Aseneth loved the best of all her seven companions was awake, and heard the sounds of crying. She was alarmed, and flew to wake up the other attendants, and all of them came to the door of Aseneth's chamber, which was locked and barred. They called to her, "What is the matter, dear mistress? Open to us and let us come in and comfort you." But Aseneth answered from within, "It is nothing but a violent headache. I am in bed, and too tired and ill to get up and open the door. Go back all of you to your beds. I shall be well to-morrow." So they dispersed to their rooms.

And when they were safely gone, Aseneth got up and opened the door of the room in which she kept her dresses and jewels, taking care to make no noise; and from among all her robes she chose out a black one which she had worn, years before, when the only son of Potipherah had died. And she cast off her royal robe and her diadem and veil and girdle, and put on the black robe and girded it with a rope. Next she went to the shrine wherein stood all the golden and silver images of her gods, and took them and threw them out of the window for the wayfarers to pick up; and she took the supper that had been laid out for her of all manner of delicate meats, and threw that into the highway for the dogs to eat. And she emptied the ashes out of the leather curtain upon the floor; she let down her hair and cast some of the ashes upon her head; she smote her breast and wept; and thus she sat in silence and misery till seven days and nights were accomplished.

And on the morning of the eighth day, when it was just dawning, and the birds had begun to twitter in the trees of the garden, and the dogs to bark at the passers-by, Aseneth raised herself a little from her crouching posture among the ashes and turned herself to the window that looked towards the east. She was faint and ill and weary from her long fasting and watching; her tongue was dry as horn, her eyes were glazed, and her fair face was haggard. She bent her head down and clasped her hands together, and crouched down again among the ashes, and said to herself, "It is all over. I have no one to turn to now. My father and mother will cast me off, for I have dishonoured their gods; they will say, 'Aseneth is no daughter of ours.' My kindred will hate me, and all the youths whom I have despised and rejected will rejoice at my humiliation; and Joseph will have nothing to say to me because I am a foul worshipper of idols. Yet," she went on to say, "I have heard that the God of the Hebrews is a merciful God, long-suffering and compassionate, not hard upon those that have sinned ignorantly, if they are sorry for what they have done. Why should I not turn to Him? Who knows if He will not have pity upon my loneliness and protect me? For they say He is the Father of the fatherless, and cares for those who are in trouble." So she rose and knelt upon her knees, with her face turned towards the east, and looked up into heaven and prayed. "Save me," she said, "from those who are pursuing me, before I am caught by them; as a little child when it is frightened runs to its father, and the father stretches out his arms and catches it to his breast, so I flee to Thee. I know that Satan, the Old Lion, is hunting me; for he is the father of the gods of Egypt, and I have insulted them and destroyed their images. I have no hope but in Thee. See, I have cast off all my beautiful robes and ornaments; I sit here in sackcloth and ashes; I have fasted and wept these seven days, because I know that I have done wrong in worshipping dumb idols, and in speaking scornfully against Joseph. But, Lord, I did it in ignorance; save me, and above all watch over Joseph, whom I love more than my own life. Keep him, Lord, in safety, and let me be his handmaid and his slave, if Thou wilt, so that I may minister to him all the days I have to live."

Much more did Aseneth say in her prayer, but it is not written down here. When she had ended, the morning star was just coming up in the east, and Aseneth rejoiced when she saw it and said, "Can it be that God has heard my prayer, and that this star is the herald of the light of the great day?" Then, in that part of the sky where the star was shining, there opened a little cleft in the heavens, and a bright light shone out of it: so dazzling that she fell on her face upon the ashes. And in the next instant there stood over her a man who was all flashing with light; and he called to her, "Aseneth, rise up." "Who can this be who calls me?" she said; "my door is barred and the tower is high. No one can have come into my chamber." So she did not look up; but the man called to her again, "Aseneth, Aseneth!" And at last she answered, "Here am I, lord: tell me, who art thou?" He answered, "I am the Prince of all the army of heaven; rise up and stand on your feet, and hear my words." Then for the first time she looked at him, and saw that he was in all things like Joseph, with royal robe, and crown and sceptre; but his face, and hair, and hands and feet were bright like the sun, and his eyes pierced like lightning; and again she was afraid, and fell on her face. But he said, "Do not be afraid; hear what I am come to say to you." Thereupon she rose and stood up, weak as she was; and he bade her go into her inner chamber and put off her black robe, and the sackcloth and ashes, and bathe herself in clear water, and array herself in the noblest of her robes, and come back to him.

Now when this was done, and she had returned to him, fresh and beautiful as formerly, he spoke kindly to her, and blessed her and said, "God has heard your prayer: He has looked upon your sorrow and tears, and has forgiven your sin. Be of good cheer, for your name is written in the Book of Life, and shall no more be blotted out. From this day forth you shall eat the bread of life and drink the cup of immortality, and be anointed with the oil of joy. And a new name shall be given you, even the name of the City of Refuge; for as you have come to God for refuge, many shall in like manner come to Him through your example by repentance. And now, behold, this day I shall go to Joseph, and tell him that which has befallen you, and he shall come to you this very day and make you his bride. Make ready therefore and array yourself in the bridal robe that is laid up in your chamber, and put upon you all your elect ornaments, and prepare yourself to meet him."

When Aseneth heard this joyful news, she fell on her face at the feet of the messenger and gave thanks to God; and, said she, "My lord, stay yet a little while, I pray you, and sit upon this couch, and I will set a table before you, and bread, and you shall eat; and I will bring you wine old and fragrant, and you shall drink, and so go on your way." For she did not know that it was an angel who had come to her. And he said, "I will do so: hasten therefore and make ready."

So first she set before him a table; and as she was going to fetch the bread he said to her, "Bring a honeycomb also." But at this she stopped, and was troubled in her mind, for she knew that there was no honeycomb in her store-room. "Why do you stop?" said the angel. "Sir," she answered, "let me send a boy to the farm which is near by, and he shall fetch you a honeycomb in a moment." "No," said he, "you need only go into your store-room, and you will find one upon the table; bring that to me." "Sir," she answered, "I know that there is none there." But he said, "Go and you will find it." She went therefore and found the honeycomb, as he had said; it was large, and as white as snow, and full of honey, and the smell of it was as the breath of life. She wondered greatly, but she would not delay, and she brought it out and put it on the table before the angel. Then he called her to him, and as she moved towards him he stretched out his right hand over her head, and again she was afraid, for she saw sparks and flashes of fire coming from it, as if it were of heated iron; so that she gazed upon him earnestly in astonishment. But he smiled and said, "You are blessed, Aseneth, for you have seen some of the secret things of God; it is of this honeycomb that the angels eat in Paradise, and the bees of Paradise have made it of the dew of the roses of life in the garden of God; and whosoever tastes it shall not die for ever." Then he put forth his right hand and took a piece of the honeycomb, and tasted it, and gave a portion to Aseneth, and she ate it; and he said, "Now you have received the food of life, and your youth shall know no old age, and your beauty shall never fade." And again he stretched forth his right hand and drew his finger across the honeycomb from the east side of it to the west, and from the north side to the south, and where his finger touched it there was left a track of the colour of blood. And immediately there came out of the honeycomb a multitude of bees. They were white like snow, and their wings were purple and scarlet, and they swarmed about Aseneth and made honey upon her lips. Among them there were some that made as though they would have stung her, but these the angel rebuked, and they fell to the ground dead. But after a while the angel said to the bees, "Go to your place," and at that they rose up in a swarm and flew out of the window and up into the sky. Then he touched with his rod the dead bees upon the floor, and said to them, "Go ye also to your place," and they came to life and flew out of the window, and settled upon the trees in the garden of Aseneth. And for the third time he stretched out his hand and touched the honeycomb upon the table, and straightway there burst forth a flame, and consumed the honeycomb—but upon the table it left no mark—and the sweet smell of the burning filled all the chamber.

Then said Aseneth, "Sir, I have seven companions, maidens who have been brought up with me, and I love them as sisters: may I not call them, and you shall bless them as you have blessed me?" So she called them in, and made them stand before the angel, and he blessed them; and thereafter he said to Aseneth, "Take away the table." And as she turned aside to lift it, he was gone. But through the window she saw in the sky a chariot and four horses shining like fire, going into the heavens towards the east, and the angel standing in the chariot. Then she said, "Ah, foolish that I am! I knew not that it was an angel out of heaven that came into my chamber, and now, behold, he is going back into heaven to his own place. Pardon me, my lord, and spare thy handmaid, for it was in ignorance that I spoke so boldly before thee!"

While she was still wondering, there came in a messenger and said, "Joseph, the mighty one of God, is on his way hither." And immediately Aseneth sent for the steward of the palace and bade him prepare a great banquet, and make all things ready; but she herself, remembering the words of the angel, went into her inner chamber and adorned herself as a bride, in shining robes, and upon her head she put a crown of gold which had in the midst, over her forehead, a great jacinth stone and six other precious stones round it; and she covered her head with a veil of wonderful beauty. Then she called to one of her maidens, who brought her a basin of pure water, and when she saw the reflection of her face in the water she was astonished at the beauty and freshness and brightness of it. Just then the steward of the palace came in to say that all was ready, and he too was struck with amazement at the sight of her, and said, "Lady, what is the cause of this wonderful beauty? Can it be that the God of heaven has chosen you to be the bride of Joseph, His elect?" And while he was yet speaking, the sound of Joseph's chariot-wheels was heard without.

Then Aseneth hastened and went down to meet Joseph, and her seven maidens followed her, and they all stood in the porch of the palace. And when Joseph saw Aseneth he also marvelled, and said, "Who art thou, maiden?" And she answered, "Thy handmaid Aseneth; and I have cast away all my idols and they are gone." And she went on and told him of the coming of the angel to her. And he rejoiced. Then they came near and embraced one another, and she led him into her father's house and made him sit on her father's throne; and Joseph said, "Let one of the maidens come and wash my feet." But Aseneth said, "No; from henceforth I am your handmaid: your hands are my hands, your feet are my feet, and your soul is my soul: none other shall wash your feet but I." So she compelled him, and washed his feet. And after that he kissed her again, and made her sit down beside him, on his right hand.

And as they were talking together, Potipherah and his wife and their household entered the palace, having returned from the country; and they were amazed, and rejoiced at the sight of Joseph and Aseneth. And when they learnt all that had happened, they rejoiced yet more; and Potipherah said, "To-morrow I will call together all my kinsfolk and prepare your marriage feast." But Joseph said, "Nay, but I will first go to Pharaoh and speak to him concerning Aseneth, that I may take her to wife; for he is to me as a father."

So on the next day Joseph departed to see Pharaoh, and forthwith Pharaoh sent for Potipherah and his wife and Aseneth; and in their presence he blessed Aseneth, and joined her hand with the hand of Joseph, and crowned them with golden crowns, and made a great feast for them lasting seven days; and all the land of Egypt rejoiced. So Joseph and Aseneth were married; and after that two sons were born to them, even Ephraim and Manasseh, in the house of Joseph.

## III

Now when the seven years of plenty were over, the years of famine began, and Jacob and his sons came to dwell in Egypt in the land of Goshen, as it is told in the Bible. Then Aseneth said to Joseph, "Let me go and see your father and greet him." So Joseph brought her to Jacob, and his brethren met him and did him obeisance at the door of the house, and they entered in. And when they saw Jacob, who was sitting upon his bed, Aseneth was struck with amazement at the sight of him, for he was noble to look upon. His head was white as snow, his beard was long, flowing over his bosom, his eyes were bright and flashing, and his muscles and limbs were those of a giant. And Aseneth fell on her face before him; and Israel said, "Is this thy wife, my son Joseph? Blessed shall she be of the Most High God." Then he called her to him, and she fell on his breast and he kissed her, and they rejoiced together. After that he inquired of her concerning her parents; and Aseneth told him how an eagle had brought her and laid her upon the altar of the temple of On; and she showed him the swaddling-clothes in which she had been wrapped. And Jacob knew that they belonged to his own daughter Dinah; and thus it was made known to him that Aseneth was of his own race, and he was the more glad.

And when they departed from him, Simeon and Levi accompanied them with the other sons of Leah and Rachel; but the sons of Bilhah and Zilpah would not go with them, for they hated Joseph. And of all Joseph's brethren, Aseneth loved Levi the most, for he was a prophet and a seer, and could read the signs of the stars of heaven.

Now it happened that as they were on their way to visit Jacob, the eldest son of Pharaoh was on the city wall, and he saw Aseneth and loved her immediately, and could think of nothing but how he might make away with Joseph and take Aseneth for his own wife. And after a few days he sent secretly to Simeon and Levi, and said to them, "I know that you are mighty men, and that with your two swords alone you defeated the men of Shechem and overthrew their city. I have sent for you because I wish to make you my friends, and, if you will do what I ask you, I will give you riches and lands and houses—in a word, all that you can desire. Now what I would have you do is this. You must know that I have been bitterly wronged by your brother Joseph: he has married Aseneth, who was betrothed to me long ago. Join with me therefore and help me to kill him, and I will take Aseneth to wife, and you shall be my brothers. If you refuse, I will slay you." And with these words he drew his sword and flourished it at them. At this Simeon, who was a man of hot temper, was enraged, and would have drawn his own sword and cut down the prince; but Levi, who could read his thoughts, trod upon his foot and made signs to him to be quiet, and whispered, "Why be angry with this fellow? We are God-fearing men, and must not render evil for evil." Then Levi said calmly and mildly to Pharaoh's son, "Why does my lord speak thus to his servants? We can do no such wickedness against our brother and against our God. Let us hear no more such evil words; but, if you will not be persuaded, know that our swords will be drawn against you." With that both the brothers drew their swords, and when the son of Pharaoh saw them he crouched upon the ground in terror, for they flashed like flames of fire and dazzled his eyes. But Levi said, "Get up and do not be frightened: only take care that you say nothing more of this kind against our brother Joseph." And they went forth from his presence.

But he could not restrain himself, for he was half-mad with anger and fear and with love of Aseneth. And after some days his servants said to him, "Do you know that the sons of Bilhah and Zilpah are at enmity with Joseph and Aseneth? They will do all that you ask of them." So he sent for them, for Dan and Gad and Naphtali and Asher, and they came to him in the first hour of the night; and after he had greeted them he sent away his servants, and said to the brethren, "Listen to me. Life and death are before you; choose which you will have: will you die like women or fight like men? I overheard your brother Joseph saying to my father Pharaoh, 'Dan and Gad and Naphtali and Asher are no brethren of mine; they are the sons of my father's handmaids, and I am only waiting till my father dies to make an end of them and their families. It was they who sold me to the Ishmaelites, and I am going to repay it into their bosom.' And my father said, 'It is well spoken: you have leave to take any of my bodyguard and deal with them as you will.'" Then Dan and Gad and their brothers were sorely troubled, and they said, "O sir, help us, and we will be your servants for ever." And he said, "I will. Hear me now: this night I will kill my father Pharaoh—for he is the helper of Joseph—and do you for your part slay Joseph. Then I will take Aseneth to wife, and you shall be my brethren and joint heirs with me in the kingdom." So they said, "We will do so, and thus it shall be: we heard Joseph say to Aseneth that she should go to-morrow into the vineyard, for it is the time of vintage. We therefore will go this night into the bed of the river and hide among the reeds; and do you take with you fifty archers upon horses, and go on before. Then will Aseneth come and fall into our ambush, and we will kill the men that are with her, and she will flee in her chariot and fall into your hands, and you shall do to her as seems good to you. As for Joseph, while he is mourning for Aseneth we will kill him; but first we will slay his children before his face." And Pharaoh's son rejoiced greatly, and sent them forth with a great body of mighty men, and they went and hid themselves in four companies among the reeds of the river on either side of the road.

Yet Naphtali and Asher murmured against their elder brothers Dan and Gad, saying, "To what purpose are you conspiring again? Did you not sell Joseph for a slave before, and, lo! he is become lord over all Egypt? Now therefore, if you imagine evil against him, he will call upon God, and fire will come down out of heaven and devour you, and the angels of God will fight against you." But their elder brothers were angry and said, "What then would you have? Are we to die like women? Not so!" And the counsel of Naphtali and Asher did not prevail with them.

In the same night the son of Pharaoh rose up and went to his father's chamber with intent to slay him, as he had promised; but when he came to the door the guards stopped him and said, "What is my lord's will?" He said, "I desire to see my father, for I am going away to-morrow to visit my vine-yard which I have newly planted." And they said, "Your father is ill and has not slept until now, and he gave us commandment that no man should come into his chamber, no, not if it were his firstborn son." So he went away in a rage, and took fifty archers with him on horses and went on before, as Dan and Gad had said.

Aseneth also arose early in the morning and said to Joseph, "Lo, I go to the vineyard as you appointed; but my soul is troubled greatly at being parted from you." But Joseph said, "Be of good cheer; the Lord is with you and will keep you as the apple of an eye. As for me, I go to distribute corn to the people of the land, that no man in Egypt may perish of hunger." So Aseneth went her way; and as she came to the place of the ambush by the river, the men that were in hiding rushed out upon her, and slew all the guard that were with her, even six hundred soldiers and fifty runners; and Aseneth fled away upon her chariot.

Now Levi, though he was afar off, saw in the spirit what was being done—for he was a seer—and told his brethren of the peril of Aseneth; and they girded every man his sword upon his thigh, and took up their shields and their spears and ran swiftly after Aseneth.

And as she fled on before, suddenly she saw the son of Pharaoh in the way, and the horsemen that were with him. Then was Aseneth in great fear, and she called upon the name of her God.

But Benjamin was in the chariot with her. Now he was a lad of nineteen years, beautiful exceedingly, and strong as a lion's whelp. And when he saw the men, he leapt down from the chariot and caught up a round stone out of the brook and threw it at the son of

Pharaoh, and smote him on the left temple, so that he fell from his horse half-dead.

Then Benjamin leapt up upon a rock by the way-side, and called to the driver of the chariot, "Give me stones out of the river bed." And he gave them; and with fifty stones Benjamin slew the fifty archers that were with Pharaoh's son; every stone smote a man on the temples.

Moreover, the sons of Leah, Reuben and Simeon, Levi and Judah, Issachar and Zebulun, pursued after the men that had laid wait for Aseneth, and fell upon them suddenly and cut them to pieces; but the sons of Bilhah and Zilpah fled before them, saying, "We are undone; and now, behold, the son of Pharaoh is dead, and all they that were with him. Let us at least slay Aseneth and Benjamin, and flee into the woods." So they pursued after Aseneth, and came upon her with their swords drawn and dripping with blood. And she was greatly afraid, and said, "Lord God, who didst save me from false gods and from the corruption of death, and didst say, 'Thy soul shall live for ever,' save me now from the hands of these wicked men!" And God heard her prayer, and straightway the swords of the men fell out of their hands and crumbled into dust.

Then they were very sore afraid, saying, "The Lord fighteth against us." And they fell down on their faces and besought Aseneth, saying, "We have imagined evil against you, and the Lord hath brought it back upon us. But now have pity upon us, and save us from the wrath of our brethren." And she said, "Go then and hide yourselves in the reeds until I appease them and turn away their anger. Only the Lord be judge betwixt me and you." Then they ran and hid among the reeds; and their brethren the sons of Leah came running like harts to overtake them. And Aseneth lighted down from her chariot and fell on their necks weeping and rejoicing; and they said, "Where are our brothers the sons of the handmaids?" that they might kill them. But Aseneth said, "I beseech you, spare them, for the Lord saved me out of their hands and broke their swords, and, behold, there they lie, like wax melted before the fire. Let it suffice you that the Lord hath fought against them on our behalf, and spare them, for they are your brethren and the sons of your father Israel." Then said Simeon, "Why doth our sister say so? Nay, but we will hew them in pieces with our swords, for they have done evil against Joseph and against our father and against thee also this day." And Aseneth took hold upon Simeon's beard and kissed him, and said, "Do not, my brother, in anywise render evil for evil: the Lord shall judge between us; and now, see, they are fled afar off. Forgive them, therefore, and spare their lives." Then Levi came near and kissed her right hand; for he knew that his brethren were in hiding among the reeds, but he would not reveal it to the others lest they should fall upon them; and he loved Aseneth because she would save them alive.

Now the son of Pharaoh, who was fallen from his horse, began to recover himself, and sat up and spat blood out of his mouth, for the blood ran down from the wound on his temple into his mouth. And Benjamin saw it, and ran and drew the sword of the son of Pharaoh (for as yet Benjamin bare no sword upon his thigh), and would have slain him; but Levi hasted and caught his hand, saying, "It is not right for us that fear God to trample upon him that is fallen, or to afflict our enemy to death. Put back the sword into its place and help me, and we will tend his wound, and if he lives he shall be our friend." Then Levi helped up the son of Pharaoh from the ground, and washed the blood from his face and bound up his wound with a bandage, and put him upon his horse and took him to Pharaoh his father, and told him all that had happened. And Pharaoh rose up from his throne and blessed Levi. But on the third day after, the son of Pharaoh died of his wound.

And Pharaoh mourned sore for his firstborn son, insomuch that he fell sick and died, being a hundred and nine years old, and left his crown to Joseph; and Joseph reigned alone in Egypt forty and eight years, and thereafter gave the kingdom to the younger son of Pharaoh, who was a sucking child when his father died. And thenceforth Joseph was called the father of the king throughout all the land of Egypt.

# JOB

This is the story of the life of Job, taken out of the book called The Testament of Job.

There came a day when Job felt that his end was near; and he called together his seven sons and his three daughters, and said to them:

Come near to me, my children, and I will tell you the story of my life, and all the dealings of the Lord with me. You must know, in the first place, that before He gave me a new name, I was called Jobab; and that I come of the family of Isaac—for I am one of the sons of Esau, Jacob's brother. Now, long ago, I used to dwell hard by the temple of an idol, and every day I saw people coming and bringing offerings, and burning sacrifices before it. But as time went on, I could not believe that this idol was indeed the God who made the heavens, and the earth, and the sea, and us men. I pondered much, therefore, upon this matter, saying, "How shall I come to know the truth of it?"

Thereafter, as I lay upon my bed, in the middle of the night, a bright light suddenly shone in my chamber, and I heard a voice calling me, "Jobab, Jobab!" (and I answered, "Here am I"). And the voice said, "Rise up, and I will tell thee that which I have to say. Verily, this idol to whom offerings are brought, and wine poured out in libations, is not a god, but is a work of the evil power whereby he deceives the sons of men." Then I bowed myself down and said, "Lord, who hast come to enlighten my soul, I beseech thee, give me leave to go and cleanse this place that is polluted by the enemy, so that offerings shall no more be made to him; but, indeed, who is there that can withstand me, seeing that I am ruler over this country?"

The voice answered me out of the light, "Thou canst indeed destroy that place; but I must forewarn thee of that which will ensue, according as I have in hand to tell thee from the Lord." And I answered, "All that He commandeth thy servant will I hear and do." And the voice said again, "If thou takest upon thee to destroy this abode of Satan's, he will rise up and fight against thee; he will bring upon thee many plagues; he will take away all thy gods; he will slay thy children. Only he will not be able to take thy life. And, if thou endurest to the end, thy name shall become famous among all generations for ever; and I will restore thee to thy former estate, and recompense thee double, and thou shalt rise up again in the resurrection of the just. Be thou therefore like a fighter who giveth blows and endureth them, looking to win the crown of victory; and then shalt thou know that the Lord is righteous, and true, and mighty, giving strength to His chosen."

And I, my children, answered him, "I will verily endure even unto death, and will not draw back." Then the angel set a mark upon my forehead, and departed from me; and in the same night I arose and gathered to me fifty of my servants, and went and destroyed the temple of the idol, laying it even with the ground. Then I returned to my house, and commanded that the doors should be made fast.

Hearken now, my children, and wonder; for as soon as I had come into my house, and had commanded the doors to be shut, and had told the keepers of the doors to say to any that came that I was not at leisure to see them, Satan came, having put on the appearance of a beggar, and said to the maid that kept the door, "Tell Job that I desire to speak with him." She came to me, therefore, and I told her again, "Tell him that I have no leisure to see him."

So Satan departed, and took on him another form, and put a wallet on his shoulder, and returned and said to the maid, "Say to Job, 'Give me bread from thine own hand, that I may eat.'" Then I took a loaf that was burnt black and gave it to the maid to give to him, saying, "Look to eat no more of my bread, for I am become a stranger to you." But the maid was ashamed to give him the burnt bread, for she knew not who he was; she took, therefore, a good loaf of her own and gave it to him. But he was aware of what had happened, and said to her, "Go back, unfaithful servant, and fetch me the bread that was given to you to give to me!" And she wept and said, "You say well that I am an unfaithful servant, for I have not done that which I was commanded." Then she brought him the burnt bread, saying, "Thus says my master, 'You shall eat no more of my bread, for I am estranged from you. This I give you only that you may not have it to say that I refused to give aught to my enemy when he asked of me.'" Satan took the bread, and sent back the maid with this message, "As this bread is burnt and blackened, so will I make thy body; in one hour I will lay thee and thy house desolate." And I answered him, "That thou doest, do quickly; for I am ready to bear whatsoever thou canst bring upon me."

Then Satan went up straightway under the firmament of the heaven, and asked of the Lord authority over me and my possessions. And the Lord granted it to him, but not at that time.

Now I must tell you, my children, of my manner of life, and my goods that I had, before I was despoiled. I had 130,000 sheep, of which 7000 were set apart for the clothing of the fatherless, and widows, and poor; and a pack of 800 dogs guarded them. I had 9000 camels; 3000 to traffic with the cities of the earth, which I laded with good things, and sent them out among the towns and villages, and had their loads distributed to the poor. I had also 130,000 asses; 500 of them were set apart that their foals might be sold, and the price given to the poor.

Also the four gates of my house were always left open to this end, that if any poor man came to beg, and saw me sitting at one of the gates, he might not turn back abashed, but might go round to another of the gates, and enter in and receive what he needed.

Within the house also I had always thirty tables ready prepared for the entertainment of strangers, and other twelve tables appointed for the widows. None left my house with his purse empty, and whenever any came to ask help, he was constrained first of all to sit down and dine. I had fifty bakehouses, and of these, twelve served the tables of the poor.

And so it was that many strangers came to my house, and some of them desired to follow my way of life and minister to the poor, but they were in need of money to furnish them therefor. And to such men I freely lent the money, taking no security of them, but only a written acknowledgment. And sometimes they prospered in their merchandise and gained money to give to the poor; but sometimes they failed and came back to me, saying, "Have patience with us." And thereupon I would destroy the bill of their debt before them, and forgive them that which they owed me.

Sometimes also there would come to me a man of a kindly heart who would say, "I have not wherewith to help the poor, but let me wait upon them to-day at your table." And at evening, when he was departing, I used to say to him, "I know that you are a labouring man, and look to your wages." And so I paid him wages for the day and let him go.

I had also psalteries and a ten-stringed lute, and every day when the widows and the poor had dined I would play to them and put them in mind of God, that they should praise Him. And if ever my handmaidens murmured at the work they had to do, I took a psaltery and sang to them of the recompense of the reward. And they were comforted, and ceased from their murmuring.

As for my children, they took part every day in the ministry, and after that they gathered together in the house of their eldest brother, and feasted there. But every morning I offered up sacrifices for them, even thirty doves, fifty kids of the goats, and twelve sheep, and a choice bullock. All of these, after I had offered up prayer, I caused to be prepared for the poor, and gave to them, saying, "Take these over and above that which you have had, and pray for my children, lest they perchance have said in their hearts, 'We are the children of a wealthy father, and these goods are ours. Wherefore should we wait upon the poor and waste our substance in this manner?'" For indeed pride is an abomination unto the Lord.

Now this was my manner of life for seven years after that the angel had come to me. But when Satan had obtained from the Lord power against me, he came down in great wrath; and first he burnt up the 7000 sheep, and 3000 camels, and 500 asses, and 500 yoke of oxen; and the rest were carried away by the men of the country to whom I had showed kindness, but now they turned against me and spoiled my goods. Then one came and told me, and I gave glory to God, and said not a word of complaint.

Satan therefore, when he saw how I took the matter, devised yet more against me, and took on him the likeness of the King of Persia, and came and spake to all the worthless men of the country, saying, "This man Jobab, who hath consumed all the good of the land, and left nothing, giving it away to the halt, and maimed, and blind, is the same that destroyed the temple of the great god and laid waste the place of offerings. It is time that he should receive the reward of his deeds. Come, fall upon him and spoil his house." But they said, "He hath seven sons and three daughters; what if they escape into other lands and accuse us of violence, and return and slay us?" Satan answered, "Trouble not yourselves for that. See, I have consumed part of his goods with fire; other part have I carried off. I will take in hand his children."

And he departed, and cast down the house upon my sons and daughters, and slew them all. And when the men saw that he had spoken truth, they came and plundered all that was in my house. Mine eyes saw worthless and dishonourable men on my couches and at my tables, and I could not utter a word, for I was stricken weak, as a sick woman. Nevertheless, I remembered the recompense of the reward; and I accounted the loss of my goods as nothing, if I might attain to that city whereof the angel had spoken.

Then there came a messenger and told me, "Thy sons and thy daughters are dead." And verily I was greatly troubled, and rent my clothes. Yet I said, "The Lord gave, and the Lord hath taken away: as it pleased the Lord, so is it come to pass: blessed be the name of the Lord."

So Satan perceived that, though all that I had possessed was taken from me, nothing could break my spirit or make me rebel against God. He departed, therefore, and asked leave of the Lord that he might afflict my body. And the Lord gave him power over my body to use it as he would, but over my life He gave him no power. Then Satan came to me as I sat upon my throne mourning for the loss of my children; and he came in the form of a great whirlwind, and cast my throne down to the ground, so that I lay for three hours without moving. And he smote me with a sore plague from head to foot, and I was filled with worms and ulcers and corruption. Therefore I arose and went out of the city in great misery and sorrow of heart, and sat upon a dunghill, being severed from the sons of men because of my evil plague. And there I remained many days. And I had no strength to work and earn my bread, so that my wife was compelled to labour as a handmaid in the house of a rich man, and carry water; and for that they gave her bread, and she brought it to me. Then was I cut to the heart, and said, "Alas for the pride of the men of this place! How can they endure to treat my wife as a slave?" Yet after that again I strengthened my soul and was patient.

After some time they refused to give my wife food enough for her and myself, but allowed her only half of what they had given her before: yet this she shared with me. Yea, she was not ashamed to go and beg of the bakers in the market-place, that she might have wherewith to feed me.

When Satan saw her do so, he took upon him the likeness of a seller of bread. And my wife came and begged of him, supposing him to be a man; and Satan said, "Pay the price, and take what you will." But she answered, "Whence should I have money? Have you not heard of all that has befallen us? If you will show mercy, show mercy; and if not, it is your own concern." He said, "If you had not deserved misfortune, I suppose it would not have come upon you; but now, if you have no money, give me the hair of your head, and take three loaves in exchange: it may be that you can live on them for three days." And she thought within herself, "What is the hair of my head to me in comparison with the hunger of my husband?" And she said to Satan, "Come, take it." And he took a pair of shears and cut off her hair, and then gave her three loaves, in the sight of all who were in the market-place. She took the bread and came to bring it to me, and Satan followed after her invisibly, and made her soul heavy within her. So, as she drew near to me she lifted up her voice and cried aloud, "Job, Job, how long wilt thou sit upon the dunghill waiting and expecting thy deliverance, while I wander about from house to house and labour as a slave? Behold, my sons and my daughters, whom I brought up with labour and pain, are perished and gone, and thou sittest under the open heaven filled with corruption, and I have to work day and night to get bread to keep thy soul in thy body. Lo, now have I sold the hair of my head for bread. Who would believe that I am Sitis, the wife of Job, who was clothed in fine linen woven with gold, that washed her feet in basins of silver and gold, that lay softly and was nurtured in plenty; but now I go barefoot, in rags, and sell my hair for bread. One thing only remains, for my bones are broken with very weariness of spirit. Arise and eat this bread, and satisfy thy hunger, and then speak a word against the Lord, and die; and I shall be freed from my misery and labour, and have rest."

But I answered her, "Lo, now these many years have I been set in the plague, enduring sickness of body and grief of heart, but my soul has never been so heavy in me as when I heard thee say, 'Speak a word against the Lord, and die.' Shall we have borne the loss of our possessions, and the death of our children, and at the end lose the true riches? Remember all the good things which we enjoyed aforetime. Shall we receive those at the hands of the Lord, and not bear to receive hard things likewise? But I perceive now why thou so speakest. Come forth, thou that standest behind her to pervert her heart and make her speak as one of the foolish women. Hide thyself no longer; come forth and withstand me to the face." Then Satan came forth from behind my wife, and stood before me ashamed, and even weeping in the bitterness of his heart; and he said, "Job, thou hast prevailed: thou art flesh and I am a spirit, but I can do no more against thee." And he departed from me in confusion. And I, my children, thought of fighters whom I had seen: one had thrown the other on the ground and filled his mouth with sand, and bruised every limb of his body, yet still he kept his hold; and of a sudden the one that was uppermost could endure the grip no longer, and gave in, so that the undermost won the crown. Thus was it with me and Satan; and, my children, I counsel you to be long-suffering in all that may come upon you; for there is nothing that is stronger than patience.

Now it was not until many years had passed that the tidings of my affliction came to the ears of the kings who were of old time my friends—for Satan caused the matter to be kept from them. But when they heard, they set forth from their countries and came to visit me, even Eliphaz of Teman, and Bildad, and Zophar, and Elihu; all of them with great trains of followers. When they were come into my land they inquired, "Where is Jobab, the ruler of Uz?" And it was told them, "He sitteth upon a dunghill without the city." And they asked what was become of my wealth—for I was aforetime richer than all the princes of the East—and they were informed of all that had befallen me. So they came where I was, and some of the men of the city with them, who showed me to them. But they said, "This is not Jobab." Yet the men of the place affirmed that it was so; and after they had disputed for some time, Eliphaz called to me, "Art thou Jobab, our fellow-king?" And I, weeping and casting dust upon my head, bowed myself in token that it was I.

Then were they stricken with great astonishment and terror, and fell to the ground as it were dead; and they rent their clothes and cast off their armour, and sat down upon the ground. And Elihu lifted up his voice and took up a lamentation over me, calling to mind all the glory of my former state, my sheep and oxen, camels and asses, my golden beds and my jewelled throne, the lamps and perfumes of my palace, and the beauty of my children, and saying, "Where is now the glory of thy kingdom?" And when he had ended his lamentation I said, "Hold your peace and I will tell you."

"My throne is in the region beyond the world, and the glory and beauty of it is at the right hand of the Father.

"This world shall pass away and the glory of it shall perish, and they that pay heed thereto shall be overwhelmed in the overthrow of it; but my throne is in the land of the holy, and the glory of it in the age that hath no change.

"The rivers shall be dried up, and the abundance of their streams floweth down into the depths of the pit; but the rivers of my land fail not, and their streams water it for evermore.

"Kings shall pass away, and rulers be no more seen: their names and their boasting shall be as the image in the glass; but my kingdom abideth for ever, and the glory thereof is as the glory of the chariot of the Most High."

Then Eliphaz waxed very wroth, and said, "Come, and let us leave him to his folly. To what purpose have we journeyed hither to comfort him, if he rails against us and says, 'Your kingdom shall be brought to nought, but mine endureth for ever'?" And he would have gone away in a rage. But Bildad restrained him, saying, "Remember that the man is sick in body and mind; we should not deal harshly with him; it may well be that he is mad." And Bildad and Zophar put questions to me to discern whether I was of sound mind or not, and I answered them soberly. And at last Zophar said, "What shall be done for thee? Behold, we have with us the most skilful physicians that are in our kingdoms. Wilt thou that they shall tend thee? Peradventure thou mayest find relief at their hands." But I said, "My healing and my medicine shall be from the Lord, who is the Maker of physicians and of all their craft."

While I was yet speaking, there came to us my wife Sitis, clothed in rags, and she had escaped by stealth out of the house of her master; for he would have kept her within, fearing that the kings would call him to account for his ill-usage of us. So when she came to us, she threw herself down before Eliphaz and said, "Rememberest thou, Eliphaz and thy fellows, how I looked and how I was attired in the former days? Look now and see in what guise I go about." And they were cut to the heart and wept, but knew not what to say; only Eliphaz took off his purple robe and put it about her shoulders. And she besought them, saying, "I pray you, command your servants to dig among the ruins of the house that fell upon our children, and seek out their bones that they may be buried and a memorial set up; for till this day we have never been able to do so because of the cost. Consider, I beseech you, what I suffer that have lost ten children, and not one of them is given to burial." So they prepared to dig; but I prevented them, and said, "Labour not in vain; ye will not find my children, for they have been taken up into the heavens by the King that created them." Again they said, "Who would not say that thou art mad? Thy children are taken up into heaven, sayest thou? Show us now what thou meanest."

I said, therefore, "Raise me up that I may stand on my feet." And they took each an arm and raised me, and I stood up and made supplication to the Father, and then said to them, "Lift up your eyes and look towards the east." And they looked, and beheld my children crowned with glory in the heavens, and above them the glory of the Most High. Which when Sitis my wife saw, she fell upon her face and worshipped, and said, "Now know I that there is remembrance of me with God. I will go now into the city and rest a little, and refresh myself for my labours of the morrow." So she went into the city, and entered into the stable of the kine that had been hers, and had been taken from her by those that employed her; and she lay down by one of the mangers and slept, having her mind at rest, and so died. And on the morrow her master sought her, and did not find her; and at last entering into the stable, he saw her lying dead there, and ran out and summoned men to him; and all the city came and saw her lying in the stable, and the beasts standing about her, lowing and making lamentation over her. Then they carried her forth and buried her beside the place of the house that had fallen upon her children.

Now as for all the words which Eliphaz, and Bildad, and Zophar, and Elihu spake with me, and those wherewith I answered them, are they not written in the book for your remembrance? Also ye know how that at the last the Lord came and answered me out of the whirlwind, and rebuked us. And we made atonement for that which we had said amiss: all but Elihu, for into him Satan had entered, and he had spoken evil words against me; wherefore he departed, and made no atonement for his sin.

Also ye know how the Lord restored to me my former state, and gave me the double of all that I had possessed before; and how I married your mother, and she bare me you: seven sons and three daughters, as it is this day.

And now behold, my sons, I die; and as for you, forget not ye the Lord, do good to the poor, pass not by the helpless, take not to yourselves wives from among the heathen.

Moreover, Job said, "I will divide my substance among you, and each of you shall possess his portion in peace."

Then Job divided his substance among his seven sons, but to his daughters he gave none of it; and they were grieved, and said, "Father, are we not also thy children?" And he answered, "Trouble not yourselves, for I have prepared for you an inheritance better than that of your brethren." And he called to him his eldest daughter, and gave her his signet-ring, saying, "Go into the treasure-chamber and bring me the three golden caskets which you will find there." And when she had brought them, he opened them, and took from them three cords, and gave one to each of his daughters. Now these cords were exceeding beautiful, of many colours, and sending forth sparks of light as it had been rays of the sun; and he said to his daughters, "Gird them about you, and keep them all the days of your life."

But Keziah, the second of the daughters, said, "Father, is this that excellent inheritance which you promised to us? What is the use of these cords? Shall we be able to live by means of them?" And he answered, "Not only so, but they will bring you even into the better life. Know ye not, my children, what is the worth of these cords? These are they which the Lord gave me on the day when He had mercy on me and healed me of my sickness; for He gave them to me, and said to me, 'Rise up, gird thy loins like a man, and I will inquire of thee and thou shalt answer Me.' And I put them about me, and straightway all my sores and plagues fell away from me, and my body was strengthened as if I had never been sick; and, moreover, I forgot all my pain and sorrow of heart. Now therefore, my children, so long as ye have these about you, the enemy can do nothing against you; no, not even to put into your minds evil thoughts. Arise, then, and gird yourselves with them before I die."

Then they did so, and their hearts were changed and renewed within them, so that they forgot the things of this world, and began to speak in the language of the angels, singing praises to the Lord of the heavens, and telling of the glory of that place and of the mighty works of the Father. And I, Nahor, the brother of Job, who wrote this testament, sat by and heard them; and that which I could I wrote down in a book, to be for them that come after, that they might know somewhat of the wonders of the Lord.

Now after three days wherein Job kept his bed—yet without pain or sickness, for no disease had power over him since the day when he put on that heavenly girdle—after three days, I say, he was aware of those that were coming to bear away his soul. And he arose, and gave to his eldest daughter a harp, and to the second a censer, and to the third an instrument of music, that they might welcome those that were on their way. And even as they took them into their hands they saw the chariots of light approaching; and they uttered hymns of praise and thanksgiving, each one in the language of them that dwell in the holy places. Then He that sat in the great chariot came near and took the soul of Job, embracing it in His arms in the sight of his daughters; but no man else saw that sight. And He took it into the chariot and departed towards the sunrising.

And after three days we made ready the body of Job to the burial;

and all the widows, and the fatherless, and the helpless came about us, crying and saying, "Woe unto us this day, woe unto us! He that was the strength of the weak, the light of the blind, the father of the fatherless, the home of the homeless, is taken from us." And they would not that his body should be hidden out of their sight. But when we carried him to the sepulchre, his three daughters went before, girded with the heavenly girdles, and giving glory to God in hymns and psalms of thanksgiving. And we laid him in the tomb as it were sleeping a fair sleep; and verily he left after him a name that shall be famous and renowned in all generations.

# SOLOMON AND THE DEMONS

In an ancient Greek book called The Testament (that is, the Last Words) of Solomon, the story is told of the way in which Solomon overcame the demons and made them serve him. The tale is put into the mouth of the king himself.

When I was engaged upon the building of the temple in Jerusalem, there was a lad, the son of the foreman of the builders, of whom I took notice, for he was a clever workman. Indeed, so skilful was he that I increased his wages and his allowance of food above the rest. Yet in spite of that, as I saw him by day, I noticed that he was becoming thin and weak and pale. So one day I called him and asked him whether anything was the matter with him. At first he would not tell me, but when I pressed him he said, "I know not whether you will believe it, O king, but a strange thing has been afflicting me. Every night when I go to my bed, something comes and sucks my right thumb, and, moreover, it steals away my food; and I feel that it is taking away all my strength, and I believe that it is an evil spirit." When I heard that, I went back to my palace, and thought earnestly, and consulted the writings of the ancients; and I prayed that a way might be shown to me how I could set the lad free from the power of the demon. And after some days there came to me an angel, and brought me a ring with a stone in it, on which was cut the figure that is called the Pentalpha and within it the Name that may not be spoken; and he told me what I must do with it. On the morrow, therefore, I sent for the lad and gave him the ring, saying, "Take this, and to-night, when the creature comes, you must cast the ring into its bosom, and say, 'In the strength of the Name, King Solomon calleth thee.' Then rise up and come running to me, and be not afraid for whatever the demon may say to you."

So that night at the accustomed hour the wicked demon Ornias came to the lad's chamber, with intent to suck his blood and take away his food. But the lad remembered my words, and cast the ring upon the demon, saying, "Come, for Solomon calleth thee," and set off at once to my palace. But the demon shrieked out after him, "Boy, what hast thou done? Take the ring from me, and I will give thee the hidden gold of the earth; take it off, and bring me not before Solomon!" But the lad took no heed; and running into the palace, he called to me, "O king, I have brought the spirit, as you told me; he is there before the door, screaming and entreating me and promising me the hidden treasures of the earth if I will not force him to come to you." Then I rose up from my throne and went out into the court of the palace, and saw the creature, in the form of a flame of fire, quivering and shrinking; and I stood over it, and said, "What is thy name?" And it answered, "Ornias." And I bade Ornias reveal to me, in the strength of the ring, how I should make him subject to me; and he told me where his abode was, and how he afflicted men, and all that I asked him. Then I sealed him with the seal of the ring, and appointed him to hew stones for the building of the temple.

Thereafter, when I had considered what I should do, I called for Ornias, and delivered the ring to him, and bade him bring before me Beelzebul, the prince of all the demons. So Ornias went to Beelzebul, and found him sitting upon his throne, and said, "Solomon calleth for thee." And Beelzebul said scornfully, "Who is this Solomon of whom thou speakest?" And Ornias cast the ring into the bosom of Beelzebul, and said again, "Solomon calleth for thee." And at that Beelzebul uttered a mighty roar, and cast forth from his mouth a great flame of fire; but he must needs rise up from his throne and follow Ornias, and stand before me. And when I saw him, I gave thanks to the Most High, who had given me power over the demons. And I spoke roughly to him; and he promised to bring before me all the demons, and that they should be subject to me, and do all that I commanded them. And I appointed him to saw blocks of marble in pieces for the work of the temple; but when the other demons saw their lord and master labouring like a slave, they shrieked aloud and were sorely dismayed.

After that I sent for many of the chief of the demons, one by one, and questioned them concerning their deeds, what diseases they sent upon men, and what secret things they knew, and how they were to be subdued; and when they had told me, I bound them, and set them to work upon the building of the temple.

Now the shapes in which they appeared before me were manifold: one was like a beautiful woman, but she had one foot like an ass's hoof; and another like a man without a head, and a flame of fire coming out of his neck; another like a great dog. These two I bound together, and the dog kept watch over the headless man, and the flame of fire that came from his neck gave light to the workmen by night. There were also dragons, one with three heads, and one with the head of a man. Another had a face that shone with a green light, and hair like serpents, but the rest of his body was darkness; and yet another was a dark man with shining eyes, and a drawn sword in his hand, who said that he was the spirit of one of the old giants who perished in the days of the flood. And of some I saw no shape, but only heard a voice. But over all of them I had dominion, and I appointed them tasks. Some I made to carry water to the builders, and some made ropes; others melted the gold and silver, and others lifted the stones. So the temple was built speedily, and I, Solomon, enjoyed great honour and peace and tranquillity in my kingdom, and the kings and princes of all the regions round about came to visit me, and brought me precious gifts; and my kingdom was greatly exalted.

Now in those days, as I was sitting on my throne in the midst of my palace (and Ornias the demon was standing by me), there came before me an old man, one of my workmen, and cast himself down before me, and cried to me to do him justice against his son; for his son ill-treated him and beat him and plucked out his hair. When I heard that, I had pity on him, for he was an old man, and weak; and I sent for his son, and asked him why he dealt so with his father. But the son denied it, saying, "I am not so given over to wickedness that I should strike my father. Be it far from me, O king: I have done no such evil." I sent him away, therefore, and called his father again, and bade him be reconciled with his son; but he said, "Nay, but let him die the death." Wherefore I was perplexed, and it was in my mind to give sentence against the young man; but it happened that I looked at Ornias the demon, and I saw that he was laughing. So I sent the people away, and said to Ornias, "Accursed one, why dost thou laugh at me?" He answered, "Forgive me, O king; it was not at thee that I laughed, but at this wretched old man: because he is contriving an evil death for his son, and, lo! in three days his son will fall sick and die." Then said I, "Is this the truth?" And he said, "It is." Then I sent for the old man and his son, and said to them, "Strive to make agreement between yourselves, and after three days come again to me; and in the meantime I will send you your food from my table." And they did obeisance and departed. And when the three days were past, I saw the old man come into the judgment-hall; and he was dressed in garments of mourning, and his face was sad. I said therefore to him, "Where is thy son?" And he answered, "I have no son: this day have I carried him to his burial."

So when he was departed, I said to Ornias, "How was it that thou knewest these things?" And he answered, "It is thus, O king. We who are spirits can fly up into the air under the firmament, and we hover about among the stars and overhear the decrees that go forth from the heavens against the children of men when they are appointed to die. But we cannot abide there for long, and so we become weak, and fall like the leaves from the trees; and when men see us they say, 'Look, there is a falling star.' But they are not in truth stars that fall, since the stars have their appointed place in the heavens, like the sun and the moon; but it is we, the spirits of the air, who are in appearance like stars." And I sent Ornias away, and marvelled greatly.

Again, in those days there came to me a letter from Adares the king of the Arabians, saying, "To King Solomon, greeting! We have heard of the wisdom that has been given to thee, and that thou art a compassionate man, and that thou hast power over all spirits that are in the air, or on the earth, or under the earth. Now be it known to thee that there is a destroying spirit in this land; for every day at dawn there arises a wind which blows for three hours, and it is so venomous that every one on whom it blows dies, and it kills the cattle also. Now therefore we entreat thee in thy wisdom to devise some means, and if it may be, send us a man who can capture the spirit; and if thou canst do so, then I and my people will be tributary unto thee, and Arabia shall keep peace with thee. And, we beseech thee, make not light of our petition, for we are in a great strait. And so farewell."

When I had read this letter, I folded it up again and gave it to my chief counsellor, saying, "Bring it again to my remembrance after seven days." Then I thought upon the matter; and after the seven days I called one of my servants and said to him, "Make ready a camel, and get an empty wine-skin." And he did so. Now the wine-skin was made of a whole hide of a beast, so that it had the upper parts of the four legs remaining upon it, the legs being sewn up, and the neck open. I said to him further, "Take this ring and go into Arabia, to the place where the venomous wind blows, and take the skin and hold the ring in front of the mouth of the skin towards the wind, so that the wind shall blow through the ring; and when the skin is blown up, you will know that the demon is inside it. Then hasten and tie up the neck of the skin, and seal it with the ring, and put it upon the camel, and bring it to me. But if on the way the demon promise you gold and silver and treasures to let him go, see that you do not obey him; but rather make him reveal to you where the treasures are hid, and mark the places, and come on to me. Now go, and good success be with you." So my servant set out and came to Arabia; and the men of the country doubted much whether he could capture the spirit. But when the day was dawning, even the first day after his coming, he rose up and set the skin with its mouth towards the wind, and laid the ring in the mouth of it; and the wind blew through the ring and entered into the skin and puffed it up. And the man caught the neck of the skin and closed it, and sealed it with the ring in the name of the Most High. Then he abode yet three days in the place to make trial of his success; but the poisonous wind blew no more, so that all the Arabians were assured that the demon was safely shut up. And they rejoiced greatly, and gave him many precious gifts, and did him great honour; and when he set forth to come back to me, they accompanied him to their borders. So he brought the skin back to Jerusalem, and put it in the midst of the temple.

Now at this time I, Solomon, was somewhat troubled, because I had a great stone made ready to be placed upon the corner of the temple, and none of my workmen and none of the demons were able to lift it and set it in its appointed place; but I was exceedingly desirous to put it there, because it was of such beauty and excellence. And on the morning after my servant was come back out of Arabia, I went down to the temple, thinking by what means I could lift the stone. And as I entered the temple I saw the skin; and it rose up and hopped seven paces, and fell on its face and did obeisance to me; and I marvelled, and bade it stand up; and it stood on its feet, puffed up with wind. Then I asked, "Who are you?" And a voice answered me from within the skin, "I am Ephippas who dwell in Arabia." And I said, "What can you do." And it answered, "I can overturn kings' palaces, and wither the green trees of the wood, and I can move mountains." Then I said, "Are you able to move this stone, and lift it up and set it upon the corner of the temple?" And it said, "Not only can I do so, O king, but if I have the demon that is in the Red Sea to help me, I can bring up the great Pillar that is there, and set it in whatever place you command." So I said, "Lift up the corner-stone." And the skin first of all became flattened, as if the wind was gone out of it, and slipped itself under the stone; and then it blew itself out again so that the stone was lifted up upon its back, and it walked upon its stumps, bearing the stone, to the ladder, and climbed up and set the stone safely in its place upon the corner of the temple; and I was greatly rejoiced, and all Jerusalem with me.

After that I sent Ephippas to fetch to me the demon that is in the Red Sea, and commanded them to bring with them the great Pillar; and after a while I saw the Pillar being borne through the air, and was astonished at the strength of the two demons. And when I considered with myself how mighty they were, and how they could shake the whole world in a moment of time, I feared to let them go; I made therefore a circle about them in the air with my ring, and said, "Stay there!" And the demons stayed, holding the Pillar sloping between heaven and earth; and there they are to this day. And if any one looks, he can see the Pillar sloping in the heavens, but the demons he cannot see. But when they let fall the Pillar, then will be the end of the world.[1]

Then I questioned the demon of the Red Sea and he told me how in old times he resisted Moses in Egypt, and helped Jannes and Jambres, the two wizards who fought against Moses; and how when Pharaoh followed after the children of Israel he went with him; and when the sea returned back and drowned the Egyptians, he was overtaken by it and shut up in the depths, and he remained there until Ephippas came and brought him to me.

Thus I, Solomon, had power over the spirits of the earth, and of the air, and of the water, and made them serve me; and my kingdom was exalted, and there was peace in my days. But when I became mighty my heart was lifted up, and I committed foolishness; for I saw the daughter of a certain Jebusite, and loved her exceedingly, and asked for her in marriage. But her kinsfolk said, "You shall not take her to be your wife except you worship our gods, even the great gods Remphan and Moloch." Then I said, "I cannot worship strange gods; why would you that I should do this?" They said, "Because they are the gods of our fathers." And I refused. Then I went to the maiden and entreated her; and she also said, "I will not hearken to you, except you worship my gods." So I departed from her. But after a little, she sent me five locusts by the hand of a messenger, saying, "Take these five locusts and crush them in the name of the god Moloch, and I will be your wife." And I did so. And forthwith my glory departed from me, and I forgot my wisdom, and became weak and foolish in my mind; and the heathen woman compelled me to build temples to the false gods, to Baal, and Remphan, and Moloch; and my spirit was darkened within me, and I became a byword among men and demons.

Therefore have I written this testament, that men might remember me, and think of their latter end as well as of their beginning.

---

[1] I believe that the Pillar is the Milky Way: it is certainly meant to be one of the constellations.

# THE STORY OF EBEDMELECH THE ETHIOPIAN, AND OF THE DEATH OF JEREMIAH

When the time was come when it was ordained that Jerusalem should be laid waste by the king of the Chaldeans, God spake to Jeremiah the prophet, saying, "Depart out of this city, for I am about to destroy it for the wickedness of them that dwell therein." But Jeremiah answered, "Suffer me, I beseech thee, Lord, to speak a word." And He said, "Say on." And Jeremiah said, "Wilt Thou indeed deliver Thy chosen city into the hand of the Chaldeans, that their king may boast himself against it and say, 'I have prevailed against the Holy City of God'? Not so, Lord; but if it be Thy will to destroy it, overthrow it rather with Thine own hand." And He said, "Neither the king nor his power shall prevail to destroy it, unless I first open the gates thereof to him. Come therefore at the sixth hour of the night to the city wall, thou and Baruch the scribe, and I will show you what I will do." Jeremiah therefore rent his clothes and put ashes upon his head, and went and found Baruch in the temple; and when Baruch saw him he was dismayed, and cried out, "What is the matter?" And when Jeremiah had told him that which was proposed concerning the city, he also rent his clothes; and they remained both of them in the holy place all that day weeping.

But at the sixth hour of the night they went out and walked upon the city wall. And suddenly they heard the sound of a trumpet in heaven, and there came down angels bearing torches of fire in their hands, and alighted upon the four corners of the wall of the city. Then Jeremiah and Baruch perceived that the desolation of Jerusalem was indeed at hand; and Jeremiah cried out to the angels, "I beseech you, destroy not the city until I have spoken a word to the Most High." So the angels stayed their hand; and Jeremiah said, "Lord, now we know of a truth that the city will be delivered into the hands of the Chaldeans; tell us, therefore, what wilt Thou that we shall do with the holy vessels of the temple?" And he answered, "Commit them to the earth, and say unto it, 'Hear, O earth, the voice of Him that separated thee from among the waters, and sealed thee with seven seals unto seven ages, even until the time wherein thou shalt be renewed in beauty: keep these vessels of the sanctuary until the coming of the Beloved.'" And Jeremiah continued and said, "I beseech Thee, show me what I shall do for Ebedmelech the Ethiopian, because he showed me great kindness and delivered me out of the pit wherein Zedekiah cast me; and I would not have him see the desolation of the city, for it would grieve him to the heart." The Lord said, "Send him to the vineyard of Agrippa which is on the other side of the hill, and I will shelter him until I bring back the people to the city. And as for thee, go thou with thy people to Babylon, and remain there to comfort them until they return hither. And let Baruch abide here until I send him word."

Then he commanded the angels, and they brake down the corners of the wall and loosened the foundations, and made weak the fastenings of the gates; and after that a great voice sounded out of the temple, saying, "Enter, ye enemies, and come in, ye adversaries; for He that kept the house hath departed from it." And the angels went up again into heaven. But Jeremiah and Baruch went into the temple, and took the vessels of the sanctuary and delivered them to the earth, as they were commanded; and forthwith the earth opened her mouth and swallowed them up. And for the rest of that night they wept and lamented; and in the morning Jeremiah called for Ebedmelech and said to him, "Take a basket and go to the vineyard of Agrippa, and fetch me some figs, that I may give them to the sick and needy among the people; and the blessing of God go with thee." And Ebedmelech set forth.

On that same morning the host of the Chaldeans surrounded the city, and a trumpet sounded in heaven, and they came against the city; and the gates gave way before them, and the wall fell, and they entered the city and laid it desolate, and took the people captive. But Jeremiah took the keys of the temple, and went outside the city and threw them up towards the sun, saying, "O sun, I say unto thee, take these keys and keep them until God shall require them of thee; for we are not found worthy to keep them any longer." And they vanished out of his sight. Then he returned, and the Chaldeans took him prisoner and carried him away to Babylon. But Baruch fled, and took refuge in a tomb, and there he remained in great sorrow of heart.

Now Ebedmelech had gathered the figs, and filled his basket; and by the time he had finished, the day had become burning hot. So he sat him down under a tree to rest a little, and then laid his head on the basket of figs and fell into a slumber. And he slept for sixty-six years without waking.

And when the sixty-six years were over, and the time of deliverance of the children of Israel was near, Ebedmelech woke up, and said to himself, "I should have been glad to sleep a little longer, for my head is still heavy; I have not slept my sleep out." And he uncovered his basket and looked at the figs, and saw that they were oozing with juice; and said again, "Well, I should like to sleep yet a little, but I am afraid I may oversleep myself; and if I do, father Jeremiah will be disappointed; for if he had not been in haste for the figs, he would not have sent me out so early." So he rose and picked up his basket of figs and put it on his shoulder, and went back to Jerusalem. When he came near the city he could not recognise it, and when he had entered the gate he could not either find his own house or see any of his acquaintance. He said therefore within himself, "Some strange delusion has come upon me; I have missed my way in coming over the hills: it must be that I was not fully awake. This will be a wonderful thing to tell Jeremiah when I meet with him." And he went out of the city. But when he looked back upon it, he could see that it was indeed Jerusalem; and he said, "It is surely the city, yet there is something wrong." He went into the city the second time, but he could find none that knew him. And he said, "God preserve me! Verily a delusion has fallen upon me," and went outside the city and sat down with the basket of figs, saying, "Here will I sit until my eyes are opened, and I can discern the truth." After some time he saw an old man coming from the fields, and said to him, "Old man, what is this city, I pray you?" The old man said, "It is Jerusalem." Ebedmelech said, "Where are Jeremiah the prophet and Baruch the scribe?" The old man answered, "You are certainly not of this city, that you inquire concerning these men. Jeremiah is in Babylon with the people that were carried away captive by Nebuchadnezzar the king." Then Ebedmelech marvelled and said, "If you were not an aged man, whom it is not lawful to mock, I should have said you were mad. How many hours is it, think you, since Jeremiah sent me to the garden of Agrippa for some figs for the sick people, and I went and gathered them and slumbered for a little under a tree, and have just now brought them back; and here they are with the juice oozing from them, just as when I picked them; and you say the people and Jeremiah are gone to Babylon!" And he opened the basket and showed the figs. And when the old man saw them he said, "Verily, my son, God has had mercy on you. He has spared you from seeing the desolation of the city. Behold, to-day it is sixty-and-six years since the people were carried away. And, if you believe not me, look upon the trees and see that it is not the time of figs." Then Ebedmelech asked, "What then is this month, and what is the day?" And he answered, "It is the twelfth day of

Nisan." And Ebedmelech believed, and gave thanks to God; and after that he gave the old man some of the figs, and bade him farewell, saying, "May God guide thee to the Jerusalem which is above." And he went to find Baruch.

And after a while he found him dwelling in a tomb; and they greeted one another, and rejoiced, and Ebedmelech told Baruch all that had happened to him, and Baruch marvelled and praised God. Then they consulted how they might send word to Jeremiah at Babylon; for they perceived that the time of the return of Israel was at hand. And it was revealed to them that on the morrow at dawn there should come a messenger whom they might send.

On the morrow, therefore, Baruch rose early and went out of the tomb, and saw an eagle sitting upon a rock hard by; and he called to it and it came, and spoke with a man's voice, saying, "I am sent hither to bear a message for thee." Baruch said, "Canst thou carry a letter to Babylon, to Jeremiah the prophet?" And the eagle said, "To that end am I sent." So they wrote a letter, and took fifteen of the figs from the basket and hung them on the eagle's neck; and Baruch blessed it, saying, "I say unto thee, O king of the birds, go in peace, and bring back an answer to me. Be not like the raven, which Noah sent out, and it returned no more to the ark; but be like the dove, which returned the third day with an answer of peace. And if the birds of the air come against thee, fight with them, and the power of God be with thee. Turn neither to the right hand nor to the left, but go straight as an arrow in the strength of the Most High."

Then the eagle flew and rested not till it came to Babylon; and there it perched upon a tree in a desert place outside the city, and waited until Jeremiah and some of the people passed by, carrying a dead man to burial. And it rose up and lighted upon the bier of the dead man, and he revived. And the eagle said to Jeremiah, "Gather the people together, and take the letter which is upon my neck, and read it in their ears." And he did so; and the people rejoiced, because the time of their deliverance was at hand. Then Jeremiah wrote a letter to Baruch, and put it upon the eagle's neck. And he blessed the eagle, and sent it away; but the figs he gave to the sick among the people. And the eagle returned to Jerusalem, and gave the letter to Baruch; and when he read it he wept, because Jeremiah had written in it all the afflictions which the people suffered at the hands of the Chaldeans.

Now when the time was fulfilled, the people were set free from Babylon, and returned to Jerusalem. And when they came back, they rejoiced and gave thanks for their deliverance for nine days. And on the tenth day Jeremiah stood up before all of them and sang a hymn of praise; and when he had ended it, he fell on the ground and became as one dead. When they saw that, Baruch and Ebedmelech lifted up their voices and wept, saying, "Our father Jeremiah, the priest of God, is departed from us!" And all the people ran together and saw Jeremiah lying as dead; and they rent their clothes and bewailed him, and then made ready to bury him. But there came a voice, saying, "Bury not the living." And at that they left off preparing a sepulchre for him, and waited, keeping watch about his body, till he should revive again.

And after three days the spirit of Jeremiah returned to him again, and he rose up and prophesied; and in his prophecy he said, "There shall be a Tree set up, which shall make the barren trees fruitful, and the proud and fruitful trees barren; and the snow shall be turned to blackness, and the sweet waters become bitter, and the scarlet shall be white as wool. Moreover, He shall bless the isles that they shall bear fruit by the word of His mouth; and He shall satisfy the hungry souls." And thereafter he began to speak to them of the coming of the Beloved into the world.

Now when the people heard it they were very angry and said, "He blasphemeth. These are the words that Isaiah spake, and they sawed him asunder with a saw of wood. Let us slay Jeremiah also, but him we will stone with stones." And Baruch and Ebedmelech cried out against them, "Do not this great wickedness!" But Jeremiah said, "Be silent, for they shall not kill me before I have delivered to you all that I have seen and heard. Fetch me a great stone." And when it was brought, Jeremiah prayed and said, "O Light of the Ages, cause this stone to appear in my likeness." And immediately the stone took upon it the likeness of Jeremiah, and the people began to stone it, believing that it was Jeremiah. And in the meantime he went on speaking to Baruch and Ebedmelech until he had committed to them all the mysteries which he had heard while he lay in a trance.

Then he arose and stood forth in the midst of the people, and the stone cried out with a loud voice, "O foolish people, why stone ye me, thinking that I am Jeremiah; and behold, he is in the midst of you!" And their eyes were opened, and they ran upon him and stoned him; and his ministry was accomplished.

But Baruch and Ebedmelech buried his body; and they took the stone and set it up over his grave, and wrote upon it, "This is the helper of Jeremiah."

# AHIKAR

## I

In the Book of Tobit in the Apocrypha you will find mention in several places of a man called Achiacharus, who was a relation of Tobit, In the first chapter (verses 21, 22) you read that he was a great officer at the court of king Esarhaddon; and at the end of the book (xiv. 10) you may learn something about his story; for Tobit says to his son Tobias, "Remember, my son, how Aman handled Achiacharus that brought him up, how out of light he brought him into darkness, and how he rewarded him again; yet Achiacharus was saved, but the other had his reward, for he went down into darkness," Then it goes on, "Manasses gave alms, and escaped the snare that was set for him, but Aman fell into the snare and perished."

Now of late years the book has come to light which tells the whole history of Achiacharus (or Ahikar, as we shall call him), and you will see as you go on that in the Book of Tobit some mistakes have been made in the names, and that instead of Aman we shall have to read Nadan, and instead of Manasses, Achiacharus.

This is the story of Ahikar. He is made to tell it himself, and he says:

When I was a young man I was steward to the great king Esarhaddon, the king of Nineveh. I was rich, and had great estates and beautiful palaces; I had everything that my heart desired, except one thing: and that was, a son. I had no child to comfort me and to inherit my great possessions after me.

Many times did I go to the temples of the gods of Nineveh and offer them sacrifices and gifts and burn incense before them; and I said, "O gods, give me a son, that I may enjoy his company while I live, and when I die he may close my eyes and bury me. And verily I am so rich that if every day from the day of my death until he died he were to take a bushel of my money and cast it away, he would not come to the end of it before his death." But the gods of Nineveh made me no answer.

Then I bethought me of the God of Israel, of whom I had learned when I was a child (for I came out of the land of the Hebrews), and I turned to Him and besought Him in like manner that He would grant me a son. And a voice came to me saying, "Forasmuch as thou hast put thy trust in false gods and sacrificed to them, thou shalt have no son. Yet this do: take thy sister's son Nadan, who is a young child, and bring him up as thine own son."

So I took Nadan and gave him to eight nurses to bring him up. He was fed on all manner of dainties, he was clothed in purple and scarlet, and slept on the softest beds. He grew up like a fair young cedar-tree; and I instructed him in all my wisdom, until I was sixty years old.

One day the king Esarhaddon returned from journeying through his kingdom, and sent for me and said, "Ahikar, my friend, my faithful and wise counsellor, you are becoming an old man. If you die, who shall succeed you and serve me in your place?" I answered, "O king, live for ever. There is with me the son of my sister, whom I have brought up as my own son, and have instructed him in all the ways of wisdom." The king said, "Go, bring him before me, and if I take pleasure in him, he shall serve me in your stead, and you can have rest from your labours, and joy and honour in your old age." So I brought Nadan to the king; and when the king saw him, he delighted in him and said, "The gods preserve you, my son!" And to me he said, "As you have served me and my father Sennacherib, so shall this youth serve me, and I will honour him and promote him for your sake." And I gave thanks to the king, and we went out, I and Nadan, from his presence. And I took Nadan home and spoke to him in private, telling him how he should conduct himself, and of what men he ought to beware, and whom he should trust. All these precepts are written in the book of Ahikar, but they are not put down here.

Now I hoped that Nadan would pay heed to my words of instruction; but when the king had exalted him, and taken him to live at the palace with him, I was grieved to see that Nadan began to become wasteful and unruly, and that, if I had suffered him, he would have squandered my money and ill-treated my servants. I admonished him, therefore, but it was in vain. He said, "My uncle Ahikar is getting old and timorous: his wisdom is failing him: one need not pay much heed to what he says." And by degrees I saw that the king began to believe Nadan, and that he no longer received me with such honour as in the old days: and this was a grief to me.

Now as I no longer had Nadan to live with me, I considered, and took his younger brother Nabu-zardan into my house. But when Nadan heard of this, he was very angry, for he thought, "Is this old man going to leave all his possessions to my younger brother, and turn me out?" So he began to think and plot how he might put me out of the way, and himself gain favour with the king.

And at last he sat down and wrote certain letters. In the first he deceitfully imitated my handwriting, and sealed it with my seal. It was written in my name to the king of Persia, saying, "From Ahikar, scribe and treasurer to Esar-haddon, king of Assyria, greeting! As soon as thou hast received this letter, set forth with thine host, and come to the plain of the south, on the 25th day of this month, and I will guide thee to Nineveh, and thou shalt take the city and possess the kingdom without any strife or battle." This letter he left lying in my chamber in the palace.

The other was written to me in the king's name, and sealed with his seal, "To Ahikar from Esarhaddon, greeting! As soon as thou receivest this letter, assemble the army, and go to the plain of the south, on the 25th day of this month; and when thou shalt see me, range the troops as if for battle, and come quickly towards me: for I have the ambassadors of the king of Egypt with me, and I desire that they should see the might of my army." This letter Nadan sent to me, and I began to make preparations as it commanded me. Thereafter Nadan took the first letter, feigning to have found it in my chamber, and brought it to king Esarhaddon. And when the king had read it, he was very angry and said, "O ye gods! what have I done to Ahikar that he should seek to betray me thus?" Nadan said, "Perhaps, my lord, it is a forgery; be not too soon disturbed; let us wait till the day appointed, and then go to the plain of the south; if Ahikar is not there, we shall know that the letter is not his; but if he is there, and armed men with him, I fear that he must indeed be conspiring against thee." And the king consented.

On the twenty-fifth day of the month, therefore, the king and Nadan set forth and rode out to the plain of the south. And I, as I had been commanded, was there with the great army which I had gathered; and so soon as I saw the king and his train approaching, I drew up the soldiers in battle array and marched quickly towards him, and the soldiers waved their weapons and shouted, and there was a great noise. Then the king was very sorely troubled, for he was sure that I had rebelled against him. But Nadan said, "Go back, my lord king, to the palace; I will capture that evil old man and bring him before you." And the king departed with his servants.

But Nadan rode up to me and said, "All that you have done is right, and well performed; the king is greatly pleased with you, and desires that you will send away the soldiers to their homes and come before him alone to receive your reward." So we rode into the city, and he brought me into the palace, where the king was seated on his throne, and all his servants about him; and I perceived that the king was in displeasure, but I knew not why. Then he put into my hand the letter which was written in my name to the king of Persia, and said, "Read that letter." And when I had read it, my knees knocked against each other, and I was speechless; I sought for a word of wisdom, but I found none. Nadan cried aloud, "O wicked and foolish old man, come forth from the presence of the king; stretch out thy hands for the cords and thy feet for the fetters!" And they bound me.

Then the king Esarhaddon turned away his face from me and spoke to Nabushemak, the chief of the executioners, who had been my friend, and said, "Take Ahikar, smite off his head, and remove it a hundred ells from his body." And I fell on my face and said, "O king, live for ever! It is thy will to slay me, yet I know that I have not sinned against thee. Now, my lord, I beseech thee, command that I may be slain before the door of my own house, and that my body may be given to my wife to be buried." And the king gave commandment accordingly.

Now as they were taking me to my house, I sent a messenger before me to my wife Ashfagni, who was a very wise woman. And she, when she heard what had happened, did not waste time in making lamentation, but hastened and prepared refreshment for Nabushemak and for the slaves that were his helpers. She came forth to meet them, and accompanied them into the house, and set food and wine before them; and the slaves drank of the wine till they were drunken and fell into a deep sleep, every one in his place.

Then I said to Nabushemak, "Do you remember how, when the father of the king delivered you to me to be put to death, I spared you because I knew that you had not done that for which you were condemned; and how, when the king learned that you were guiltless, he took you into favour again, and rewarded me? Now I swear to you that I likewise have not conspired against king Esarhaddon, but I have been falsely accused. Save me therefore; but lest the rumour should be spread abroad that I have not been put to death, do this. I have a prisoner in my house who is condemned justly to death. Take my clothes and put them upon him, and smite off his head; behold, your servants are drunken and will perceive nothing, and I will be in hiding until the day when the truth is made known."

And Nabushemak was glad—for he was my friend—and agreed; and it was done as I advised. The slaves took the prisoner and smote off his head, perceiving nothing, and gave his body to be buried instead of me; and it was published throughout all Nineveh and Assyria that Ahikar was dead.

Then Nabushemak and my wife Ashfagni made a hiding-place in the ground; it was four cubits long and three broad and five in height, and it was covered with a stone. There they hid me, and gave me bread and water to eat, secretly, and there I abode many days. But Esarhaddon was grieved in spirit, and said to Nadan, "Go to the house of Ahikar and celebrate his funeral, for he was thy uncle, and served me and my father faithfully for a long time." So Nadan came to my house; but he did not celebrate my funeral. He gathered together strange men and women, and feasted with them, and sang, and drank, and was drunken. He mocked at my wife Ashfagni, and as for my servants, who loved me and had been long in my house, he stripped them and beat them and ill-treated them until I heard the voice of their weeping and crying in my hiding-place, and I prayed the Most High to deliver us and to reward Nadan according to his works.

## II

Now when Pharaoh, king of Egypt, heard that I, Ahikar, was dead, he was very glad; for he had always stood in awe of my wisdom. And he wrote a letter to Esarhaddon in these words: "Pharaoh, king of Egypt, to Esarhaddon, king of Assyria, greeting! I desire to build a castle between heaven and earth. Send me therefore a wise man to whom I may commit the business. If he accomplishes all that I require and answers all my questions, I will send you by his hands the whole revenue of Egypt for three years. But if you cannot send me such a man, then you must send to me, by my messenger, the whole revenue of Assyria for three years. And if not, I shall come against you and lay your land desolate. And so farewell."

When the letter was read before Esarhaddon, he called together his princes and counsellors and wise men, and said to them, "Which of you will go to Egypt and answer the questions of Pharaoh?" They said, "Lord and king, in the time of your father it was Ahikar the scribe who answered all hard questions and solved all difficulties; and behold, now you have with you his sister's son Nadan, who has been instructed in his wisdom and can do all that you require." So the king turned to Nadan and said, "Will you go to Egypt and answer Pharaoh?" But Nadan said, "It is folly! The gods themselves could not build a castle between heaven and earth; how then should the children of men accomplish such a thing?" When the king heard that, he arose and came down from his throne, and threw himself on the ground lamenting and saying, "Alas, alas, I am undone. I have slain my servant Ahikar at the word of a foolish boy, and there is none like him left! Who can give him back to me?"

Then Nabushemak spoke and said, "O king, live for ever. He that disobeys the commandments of his master is worthy of death. Say therefore the word, and let them hang me on a tree; for Ahikar, whom you bade me slay, is not dead, but living!" The king said, "O Nabushemak, if it be as you say, and if you can show me Ahikar alive, I will give you ten thousand talents of gold and a hundred robes of purple. Say on, therefore." Nabushemak said, "One thing I ask of my lord: that he will not keep this my trespass in mind, nor store up wrath against me." And the king sware to him.

Nabushemak went forth immediately and mounted his chariot, and drove swiftly to my house. He uncovered the hiding-place and brought me forth, and took me up into his chariot and led me into the presence of the king. And when the king saw me, he wept; for I was in evil plight. My hair was grown over my shoulders, and my beard reached down to my girdle; my body was foul with dirt, and my nails were as long as eagles' claws; my eyes were dim from the darkness, and my limbs were stiff so that I could scarcely walk. And the king said, "O Ahikar, it is not I that have brought this misery upon you, but he whom you have brought up as your own son." I answered, "O king, since mine eyes have looked upon you I have no more sorrow or pain." The king said, "Go to your house, bathe your body, and cut your hair; refresh yourself and take your rest for forty days; then come back to me." And I did so. But after twenty days I had recovered my strength, and I went back to the king. Then he showed me the letter of the king of Egypt, saying, "Behold, Ahikar, the burden which they would lay upon me and upon my kingdom." And I answered, "O king, live for ever. Trouble not yourself, nor be disquieted about this matter. I will go to Egypt and answer the hard questions; and I will bring back to you the revenues of Egypt for three years." So the king was comforted; he rejoiced greatly, and made a feast, and gave me rich presents.

Immediately after this, I began to make ready for my journey; and first I ordered my huntsmen to catch two young eagles alive. I also chose from among my servants two young boys whose names were Nabuchal and Tabshalom, and taught them to ride upon the backs of the eagles; and after a while the eagles became accustomed to bear them up in the air. I also taught them certain words which they should say at the appointed time, and practised them until they knew perfectly what they had to do.

And when all was prepared, I set forth with a great company and went to Egypt. It was told Pharaoh that an embassy was come from Nineveh, and he sent for me, and when I appeared before him he asked who I was. And I answered, "I am Abikam, one of the least of the servants of Esar-haddon." Pharaoh was displeased, and said, "Am I then so much despised by your master that he sends me the least of his servants?" I said, "My lord Esarhaddon is so far exalted above his servants that in his sight the great and the small are all alike." He said, "Depart from my presence, and to-morrow come again to me."

Then Pharaoh, who desired foolishly to make himself appear great in our eyes, arrayed himself in purple, and made his nobles put on scarlet and stand about him; and when I came into his presence he asked me to what I compared him. I said, "My lord, you are like the god Bel, and your nobles are like his priests." And in like manner on the following days he dressed himself in various colours, and each day asked me what I should liken him to. And I said, "To the sun" on one day, and "To the moon" on the next, and on the third day, "To the spring and the flowers of it." And he was greatly pleased, and said, "Abikam, you have compared me to the god Bel, and to the sun and the moon and the spring; now tell me, to what do you liken your master Esarhaddon?" I said, "I cannot tell you, O king, until you have risen from your throne." So Pharaoh stood up, and I said, "My lord Esarhaddon is like the great God of Heaven in respect of you: He has dominion over the god Bel, He can forbid the sun to shine and the moon to rise, and He can lay waste the spring and all the flowers thereof." Then Pharaoh was displeased and said, "I adjure you by the life of your lord Esarhaddon, tell me, what is your name, in very deed?" I answered, "I am Ahikar the scribe, and the seal of Esarhaddon is in my keeping."

Pharaoh was troubled when he learned that I was yet alive, and he sent me away, saying, "Tomorrow come to me and tell me a thing which neither I nor my nobles have ever heard." So I took thought, and wrote in the name of Pharaoh a bond in which it was said that he owed to my lord Esarhaddon nine hundred talents of gold. And next day I brought it before Pharaoh; but before I had opened it the nobles cried out, saying, "We know it of old, we know it well!" Then said I, "I thank you for acknowledging the debt." And I gave the paper to the king, and he looked on it and said to them, "What! Do you acknowledge that I owe nine hundred talents of gold to Esarhaddon?" And they were confounded, and cried out again, "No! no! we have never heard of any such thing." So I said, "If it be so, I have done what you required."

But Pharaoh said, "It is enough: I have sent for you to build me a castle between the earth and the heavens; even a thousand cubits above the earth. Come forth into the plain to-morrow and accomplish this." And I said, "Well, O king; and do you for your part bring masons and that which is necessary for building." So on the morrow a great multitude assembled to see how the matter would go. But I had my eagles and my boys in readiness; and when Pharaoh gave the word, I sent them up, the boys riding on the eagles; and when they were high up in the air, the boys called out, as I had taught them, "Bring us mortar, lime, and stones: we are ready to begin the building!" And the masons and all the people were amazed, gaping at the boys. And I fell upon the masons and beat them, saying, "Why delay you? Make haste, give them what they ask for," and such-like words, till they fled before me. And I said to Pharaoh, "If your people refuse to do their part, how can I do mine?" And Pharaoh and his nobles murmured, but they could not think of any answer. So Pharaoh said, "It is enough; leave the matter of the castle; I have other questions to ask you."

On the morrow he called for me, and said, "I saw a great pillar built of 8763 bricks, and about it are planted twelve cedars, and each has thirty branches, and on each branch are a black and a white mouse which gnaw it." I laughed and made answer, "O king, there is not a child in the land of Assyria who could not interpret this riddle. The pillar is the year, the bricks are the hours, the cedars the months, their branches the days, and the black and white mice are the night and the day."

Pharaoh's face fell, and he said, "Well. But now I command you to plait me a rope out of the sand." I answered, "Let them bring me a pattern out of your store-house, O king, that I may have it to copy." He said, "You trifle with me; and unless you plait me such a rope I will not pay you the revenues of Egypt." I went aside therefore and considered; and knowing that the Egyptians were foolish, I thought upon a plan. I got a mass of sand and put it in a chest, and made it run out through two pipes so that when the sun shone upon it, it appeared like the strands of a rope; and I called to the king, "Let your servants plait together the two strands of the rope which I have made, and when they have done so I will make more." And again they were dismayed, and could say nothing.

Lastly, Pharaoh showed me a millstone which was broken in two pieces, and said, "Come, Ahikar, sew this together for me." But I took a small piece of a like stone, and said, "O king, I have not my tools with me; but command your shoemaker to cut me a thread out of this piece of stone, and I will sew the millstone together forthwith." Then Pharaoh laughed, and said, "Well, Ahikar, it was on a good day for your lord that you were born. Come, I will make you a feast, and after that you shall return to your own land."

So after certain days I departed, taking with me the revenues of Egypt for three years, and also the nine hundred talents which I had made Pharaoh acknowledge that he owed to my lord. And Esar-haddon came forth to meet me; and when he heard what I had done, he made me sit down on his right hand, and said, "Ahikar, ask what thou wilt and I will give it thee." Then I said, "O king, live for ever! Two things only will I require of thee: one, that thou wouldst do good unto Nabushemak, for it is by his means that I was saved alive; and the other, that thou wouldst give me power over my sister's son Nadan, and not require his life at my hand." And the king granted my request, and exalted Nabushemak to the first rank in his kingdom; but Nadan he delivered into my hand.

I took Nadan to the hall of my house, and set him with his feet in the stocks, and a collar of iron about his neck, and iron bands upon his hands; I fed him with bread and water, and chastised him with rods. And when I came in or out of my house I stood and reproached him, speaking in parables and proverbs.

Now these are some of the parables which I spake to Nadan:

"My son, thou art like one that shot an arrow into the heaven to slay God: the arrow fell back upon him and pierced him."

"Thou art like one that saw his neighbour shivering with cold, and took a vessel of cold water and poured it over him."

"Thou didst think to take my place after my death; but know that even if the tail of the pig grew seven cubits long, no man would mistake the pig for a horse."

"Thou art like the trap that was set on a dunghill. The sparrow saw it and said, 'Brother, what dost thou here?' The trap answered, 'I am fasting and praying.' The sparrow said, 'And what is that piece of wood by thee?' The trap said, 'My staff upon which I lean when I pray.' 'And what is that in thy mouth?' 'It is a little food for hungry wayfarers.' Then said the sparrow, 'I am hungry and a wayfarer.' 'Come hither then,' said the trap, 'and fear nothing.' But when the sparrow came, the trap caught it by the head; and the sparrow said, 'If these be thy fastings and prayers, God will not accept thy fasting nor hearken to thy prayer.'"

"Thou art like the pig that went to the bath along with the nobles; and when it had bathed and come forth, it saw a pool of mud, and went and rolled therein."

"Hearken: a serpent was sleeping on a thorn-bush, and a flood came and swept them both away. And a wolf saw them floating on the water, and said, 'There goes one evil upon another evil, and a third evil carrying them off.' The serpent said, 'And dost thou bring back the kids and lambs to their mothers?' 'Nay,' said the wolf. The serpent said, 'I know not whether there is much to choose betwixt us.'"

"Thou art like the mole that came up out of the ground to curse God because He had not given to it sharpness of sight; and the eagle saw it, and carried it off."

"When men say to the wolf, 'Get away from the flock,' he saith, 'Nay, but the dust thereof is healing to mine eyes.' When they took him to the school, the teacher said, 'Say A.' The wolf said, 'Lamb.' 'Say B.' He answered, 'Kid.' Surely he spake of that which was in his thoughts."

At last, after many days, Nadan besought me, saying, "Have mercy on me, spare my life, and I will feed thy swine and keep thine asses, and be thy slave for ever."

And I said, "Thou art like the palm-tree which bare no dates, and the owner came to cut it down; and it said, 'Leave me this one year, and next year I will bear melons.' But he said, 'Thou that hast not borne thine own fruit, how wilt thou bear one that is not thine?' Now, behold, I will say no more to thee, O Nadan; but let God, who preserved me alive, judge between thee and me."

And forthwith judgment went forth against Nadan, and his body swelled up and burst, and he died. For it is written, "He that diggeth a pit for another shall fall into the midst of it himself."

## THE END

# A THIN GHOST

# AND OTHERS

## PREFACE

Two of these stories, the third and fourth, have appeared in print in the Cambridge Review, and I wish to thank the proprietor for permitting me to republish them here.

I have had my doubts about the wisdom of publishing a third set of tales; sequels are, not only proverbially but actually, very hazardous things. However, the tales make no pretence but to amuse, and my friends have not seldom asked for the publication. So not a great deal is risked, perhaps, and perhaps also some one's Christmas may be the cheerfuller for a storybook which, I think, only once mentions the war.

# A THIN GHOST AND OTHERS

## THE RESIDENCE AT WHITMINSTER

Dr. Ashton—Thomas Ashton, Doctor of Divinity—sat in his study, habited in a dressing-gown, and with a silk cap on his shaven head—his wig being for the time taken off and placed on its block on a side table. He was a man of some fifty-five years, strongly made, of a sanguine complexion, an angry eye, and a long upper lip. Face and eye were lighted up at the moment when I picture him by the level ray of an afternoon sun that shone in upon him through a tall sash window, giving on the west. The room into which it shone was also tall, lined with book-cases, and, where the wall showed between them, panelled. On the table near the doctor's elbow was a green cloth, and upon it what he would have called a silver standish—a tray with inkstands—quill pens, a calf-bound book or two, some papers, a churchwarden pipe and brass tobacco-box, a flask cased in plaited straw, and a liqueur glass. The year was 1730, the month December, the hour somewhat past three in the afternoon.

I have described in these lines pretty much all that a superficial observer would have noted when he looked into the room. What met Dr. Ashton's eye when he looked out of it, sitting in his leather arm-chair? Little more than the tops of the shrubs and fruit-trees of his garden could be seen from that point, but the red brick wall of it was visible in almost all the length of its western side. In the middle of that was a gate—a double gate of rather elaborate iron scroll-work, which allowed something of a view beyond. Through it he could see that the ground sloped away almost at once to a bottom, along which a stream must run, and rose steeply from it on the other side, up to a field that was park-like in character, and thickly studded with oaks, now, of course, leafless. They did not stand so thick together but that some glimpse of sky and horizon could be seen between their stems. The sky was now golden and the horizon, a horizon of distant woods, it seemed, was purple.

But all that Dr. Ashton could find to say, after contemplating this prospect for many minutes, was: "Abominable!"

A listener would have been aware, immediately upon this, of the sound of footsteps coming somewhat hurriedly in the direction of the study: by the resonance he could have told that they were traversing a much larger room. Dr. Ashton turned round in his chair as the door opened, and looked expectant. The incomer was a lady—a stout lady in the dress of the time: though I have made some attempt at indicating the doctor's costume, I will not enterprise that of his wife—for it was Mrs. Ashton who now entered. She had an anxious, even a sorely distracted, look, and it was in a very disturbed voice that she almost whispered to Dr. Ashton, putting her head close to his, "He's in a very sad way, love, worse, I'm afraid." "Tt—tt, is he really?" and he leaned back and looked in her face. She nodded. Two solemn bells, high up, and not far away, rang out the half-hour at this moment. Mrs. Ashton started. "Oh, do you think you can give order that the minster clock be stopped chiming to-night? 'Tis just over his chamber, and will keep him from sleeping, and to sleep is the only chance for him, that's certain." "Why, to be sure, if there were need, real need, it could be done, but not upon any light occasion. This Frank, now, do you assure me that his recovery stands upon it?" said Dr. Ashton: his voice was loud and rather hard. "I do verily believe it," said his wife. "Then, if it must be, bid Molly run across to Simpkins and say on my authority that he is to stop the clock chimes at sunset: and—yes—she is after that to say to my lord Saul that I wish to see him presently in this room." Mrs. Ashton hurried off.

Before any other visitor enters, it will be well to explain the situation.

Dr. Ashton was the holder, among other preferments, of a prebend in the rich collegiate church of Whitminster, one of the foundations which, though not a cathedral, survived dissolution and reformation, and retained its constitution and endowments for a hundred years after the time of which I write. The great church, the residences of the dean and the two prebendaries, the choir and its appurtenances, were all intact and in working order. A dean who flourished soon after 1500 had been a great builder, and had erected a spacious quadrangle of red brick adjoining the church for the residence of the officials. Some of these persons were no longer required: their offices had dwindled down to mere titles, borne by clergy or lawyers in the town and neighbourhood; and so the houses that had been meant to accommodate eight or ten people were now shared among three, the dean and the two prebendaries. Dr. Ashton's included what had been the common parlour and the dining-hall of the whole body. It occupied a whole side of the court, and at one end had a private door into the minster. The other end, as we have seen, looked out over the country.

So much for the house. As for the inmates, Dr. Ashton was a wealthy man and childless, and he had adopted, or rather undertaken to bring up, the orphan son of his wife's sister. Frank Sydall was the lad's name: he had been a good many months in the house. Then one day came a letter from an Irish peer, the Earl of Kildonan (who had known Dr. Ashton at college), putting it to the doctor whether he would consider taking into his family the Viscount Saul, the Earl's heir, and acting in some sort as his tutor. Lord Kildonan was shortly to take up a post in the Lisbon Embassy, and the boy was unfit to make the voyage: "not that he is sickly," the Earl wrote, "though you'll find him whimsical, or of late I've thought him so, and to confirm this, 'twas only to-day his old nurse came expressly to tell me he was possess'd: but let that pass; I'll warrant you can find a spell to make all straight. Your arm was stout enough in old days, and I give you plenary authority to use it as you see fit. The truth is, he has here no boys of his age or quality to consort with, and is given to moping about in our raths and graveyards: and he brings home romances that fright my servants out of their wits. So there are you and your lady forewarned." It was perhaps with half an eye open to the possibility of an Irish bishopric (at which another sentence in the Earl's letter seemed to hint) that Dr. Ashton accepted the charge of my Lord Viscount Saul and of the 200 guineas a year that were to come with him.

So he came, one night in September. When he got out of the chaise that brought him, he went first and spoke to the postboy and gave him some money, and patted the neck of his horse. Whether he made some movement that scared it or not, there was very nearly a nasty accident, for the beast started violently, and the postilion being unready was thrown and lost his fee, as he found afterwards, and the chaise lost some paint on the gateposts, and the wheel went over the man's foot who was taking out the baggage. When Lord Saul came up the steps into the light of the lamp in the porch to be greeted by Dr. Ashton, he was seen to be a thin youth of, say, sixteen years old, with straight black hair and the pale colouring that is common to such a figure. He took the accident and commotion calmly enough, and expressed a proper anxiety for the people who had been, or might have been, hurt: his voice was smooth and pleasant, and without any trace, curiously, of an Irish brogue.

Frank Sydall was a younger boy, perhaps of eleven or twelve, but Lord Saul did not for that reject his company. Frank was able to teach him various games he had not known in Ireland, and he was apt at learning them; apt, too, at his books, though he had had little or no regular teaching at home. It was not long before he was making a shift to puzzle out the inscriptions on the tombs in the minster, and he would often put a question to the doctor about the old books in the library that required some thought to answer. It is to be supposed that he made himself very agreeable to the servants, for within ten days of his coming they were almost falling over each other in their efforts to oblige him. At the same time, Mrs. Ashton was rather put to it to find new maidservants; for there were several changes, and some of the families in the town from which she had been accustomed to draw seemed to have no one available. She was forced to go further afield than was usual.

These generalities I gather from the doctor's notes in his diary and from letters. They are generalities, and we should like, in view of what has to be told, something sharper and more detailed. We get it in entries which begin late in the year, and, I think, were posted up all together after the final incident; but they cover so few days in all that there is no need to doubt that the writer could remember the course of things accurately.

On a Friday morning it was that a fox, or perhaps a cat, made away with Mrs. Ashton's most prized black cockerel, a bird without a single white feather on its body. Her husband had told her often enough that it would make a suitable sacrifice to Æsculapius; that had discomfited her much, and now she would hardly be consoled. The boys looked everywhere for traces of it: Lord Saul brought in a few feathers, which seemed to have been partially burnt on the garden rubbish-heap. It was on the same day that Dr. Ashton, looking out of an upper window, saw the two boys playing in the corner of the garden at a game he did not understand. Frank was looking earnestly at something in the palm of his hand. Saul stood behind him and seemed to be listening. After some minutes he very gently laid his hand on Frank's head, and almost instantly thereupon, Frank suddenly dropped whatever it was that he was holding, clapped his hands to his eyes, and sank down on the grass. Saul, whose face expressed great anger, hastily picked the object up, of which it could only be seen that it was glittering, put it in his pocket, and turned away, leaving Frank huddled up on the grass. Dr. Ashton rapped on the window to attract their attention, and Saul looked up as if in alarm, and then springing to Frank, pulled him up by the arm and led him away. When they came in to dinner, Saul explained that they had been acting a part of the tragedy of Radamistus, in which the heroine reads the future fate of her father's kingdom by means of a glass ball held in her hand, and is overcome by the terrible events she has seen. During this explanation Frank said nothing, only looked rather bewilderedly at Saul. He must, Mrs. Ashton thought, have contracted a chill from the wet of the grass, for that evening he was certainly feverish and disordered; and the disorder was of the mind as well as the body, for he seemed to have something he wished to say to Mrs. Ashton, only a press of household affairs prevented her from paying attention to him; and when she went, according to her habit, to see that the light in the boys' chamber had been taken away, and to bid them good-night, he seemed to be sleeping, though his face was unnaturally flushed, to her thinking: Lord Saul, however, was pale and quiet, and smiling in his slumber.

Next morning it happened that Dr. Ashton was occupied in church and other business, and unable to take the boys' lessons. He therefore set them tasks to be written and brought to him. Three times, if not oftener, Frank knocked at the study door, and each time the doctor chanced to be engaged with some visitor, and sent the boy off rather roughly, which he later regretted. Two clergymen were at dinner this day, and both remarked—being fathers of families—that the lad seemed sickening for a fever, in which they were too near the truth, and it had been better if he had been put to bed forthwith: for a couple of hours later in the afternoon he came running into the house, crying out in a way that was really terrifying, and rushing to Mrs. Ashton, clung about her, begging her to protect him, and saying, "Keep them off! keep them off!" without intermission. And it was now evident that some sickness had taken strong hold of him. He was therefore got to bed in another chamber from that in which he commonly lay, and the physician brought to him: who pronounced the disorder to be grave and affecting the lad's brain, and prognosticated a fatal end to it if strict quiet were not observed, and those sedative remedies used which he should prescribe.

We are now come by another way to the point we had reached before. The minster clock has been stopped from striking, and Lord Saul is on the threshold of the study.

"What account can you give of this poor lad's state?" was Dr. Ashton's first question. "Why, sir, little more than you know already, I fancy. I must blame myself, though, for giving him a fright yesterday when we were acting that foolish play you saw. I fear I made him take it more to heart than I meant." "How so?" "Well, by telling him foolish tales I had picked up in Ireland of what we call the second sight." "Second sight! What kind of sight might that be?" "Why, you know our ignorant people pretend that some are able to foresee what is to come—sometimes in a glass, or in the air, maybe, and at Kildonan we had an old woman that pretended to such a power. And I daresay I coloured the matter more highly than I should: but I never dreamed Frank would take it so near as he did." "You were wrong, my lord, very wrong, in meddling with such superstitious matters at all, and you should have considered whose house you were in, and how little becoming such actions are to my character and person or to your own: but pray how came it that you, acting, as you say, a play, should fall upon anything that could so alarm Frank?" "That is what I can hardly tell, sir: he passed all in a moment from rant about battles and lovers and Cleodora and Antigenes to something I could not follow at all, and then dropped down as you saw." "Yes: was that at the moment when you laid your hand on the top of his head?" Lord Saul gave a quick look at his questioner—quick and spiteful—and for the first time seemed unready with an answer. "About that time it may have been," he said. "I have tried to recollect myself, but I am not sure. There was, at any rate, no significance in what I did then." "Ah!" said Dr. Ashton, "well, my lord, I should do wrong were I not to tell you that this fright of my poor nephew may have very ill consequences to him. The doctor speaks very despondingly of his state." Lord Saul pressed his hands together and looked earnestly upon Dr. Ashton. "I am willing to believe you had no bad intention, as assuredly you could have no reason to bear the poor boy malice: but I cannot wholly free you from blame in the affair." As he spoke, the hurrying steps were heard again, and Mrs. Ashton came quickly into the room, carrying a candle, for the evening had by this time closed in. She was greatly agitated. "O come!" she cried, "come directly. I'm sure he is going." "Going? Frank? Is it possible? Already?" With some such incoherent words the doctor caught up a book of prayers from the table and ran out after his wife. Lord Saul stopped for a moment where he was. Molly, the maid, saw him bend over and put both hands to his face. If it were the last words she had to speak, she said afterwards, he was striving to keep back a fit of laughing. Then he went out softly, following the others.

Mrs. Ashton was sadly right in her forecast. I have no inclination to imagine the last scene in detail. What Dr. Ashton records is, or may be taken to be, important to the story. They asked Frank if he would like to see his companion, Lord Saul, once again. The boy was quite collected, it appears, in these moments. "No," he said, "I do not want to see him; but you should tell him I am afraid he will be very cold." "What do you mean, my dear?" said Mrs. Ashton. "Only that;" said Frank, "but say to him besides that I am free of them now, but he should take care. And I am sorry about your black cockerel, Aunt Ashton; but he said we must use it so, if we were to see all that could be seen."

Not many minutes after, he was gone. Both the Ashtons were grieved, she naturally most; but the doctor, though not an emotional man, felt the pathos of the early death: and, besides, there was the growing suspicion that all had not been told him by Saul, and that there was something here which was out of his beaten track. When he left the chamber of death, it was to walk across the quadrangle of the residence to the sexton's house. A passing bell, the greatest of the minster bells, must be rung, a grave must be dug in the minster yard, and there was now no need to silence the chiming of the minster clock. As he came slowly back in the dark, he thought he must see Lord Saul again. That matter of the black cockerel—trifling as it might seem—would have to be cleared up. It might be merely a fancy of the sick boy, but if not, was there not a witch-trial he had read, in which some grim little rite of sacrifice had played a part? Yes, he must see Saul.

I rather guess these thoughts of his than find written authority for them. That there was another interview is certain: certain also that Saul would (or, as he said, could) throw no light on Frank's words: though the message, or some part of it, appeared to affect him horribly. But there is no record of the talk in detail. It is only said that Saul sat all that evening in the study, and when he bid good-night, which he did most reluctantly, asked for the doctor's prayers.

The month of January was near its end when Lord Kildonan, in the Embassy at Lisbon, received a letter that for once gravely disturbed that vain man and neglectful father. Saul was dead. The scene at Frank's burial had been very distressing. The day was awful in blackness and wind: the bearers, staggering blindly along under the flapping black pall, found it a hard job, when they emerged from the porch of the minster, to make their way to the grave. Mrs. Ashton was in her room—women did not then go to their kinsfolk's funerals—but Saul was there, draped in the mourning cloak of the time, and his face was white and fixed as that of one dead, except when, as was noticed three or four times, he suddenly turned his head to the left and looked over his shoulder. It was then alive with a terrible expression of listening fear. No one saw him go away: and no one could find him that evening. All night the gale buffeted the high windows of the church, and howled over the upland and roared through the woodland. It was useless to search in the open: no voice of shouting or cry for help could possibly be heard. All that Dr. Ashton could do was to warn the people about the college, and the town constables, and to sit up, on the alert for any news, and this he did. News came early next morning, brought by the sexton, whose business it was to open the church for early prayers at seven, and who sent the maid rushing upstairs with wild eyes and flying hair to summon her master. The two men dashed across to the south door of the minster, there to find Lord Saul clinging desperately to the great ring of the door, his head sunk between his shoulders, his stockings in rags, his shoes gone, his legs torn and bloody.

This was what had to be told to Lord Kildonan, and this really ends the first part of the story. The tomb of Frank Sydall and of the Lord Viscount Saul, only child and heir to William Earl of Kildonan, is one: a stone altar tomb in Whitminster churchyard.

Dr. Ashton lived on for over thirty years in his prebendal house, I do not know how quietly, but without visible disturbance. His successor preferred a house he already owned in the town, and left that of the senior prebendary vacant. Between them these two men saw the eighteenth century out and the nineteenth in; for Mr. Hindes, the successor of Ashton, became prebendary at nine-and-twenty and died at nine-and-eighty. So that it was not till 1823 or 1824 that any one succeeded to the post who intended to make the house his home. The man who did was Dr. Henry Oldys, whose name may be known to some of my readers as that of the author of a row of volumes labelled Oldys's Works, which occupy a place that must be honoured, since it is so rarely touched, upon the shelves of many a substantial library.

Dr. Oldys, his niece, and his servants took some months to transfer furniture and books from his Dorsetshire parsonage to the quadrangle of Whitminster, and to get everything into place. But eventually the work was done, and the house (which, though untenanted, had always been kept sound and weather-tight) woke up, and like Monte Cristo's mansion at Auteuil, lived, sang, and bloomed once more. On a certain morning in June it looked especially fair, as Dr. Oldys strolled in his garden before breakfast and gazed over the red roof at the minster tower with its four gold vanes, backed by a very blue sky, and very white little clouds.

"Mary," he said, as he seated himself at the breakfast table and laid down something hard and shiny on the cloth, "here's a find which the boy made just now. You'll be sharper than I if you can guess what it's meant for." It was a round and perfectly smooth tablet—as much as an inch thick—of what seemed clear glass. "It is rather attractive at all events," said Mary: she was a fair woman, with light hair and large eyes, rather a devotee of literature. "Yes," said her uncle, "I thought you'd be pleased with it. I presume it came from the house: it turned up in the rubbish-heap in the corner." "I'm not sure that I do like it, after all," said Mary, some minutes later. "Why in the world not, my dear?" "I don't know, I'm sure. Perhaps it's only fancy." "Yes, only fancy and romance, of course. What's that book, now—the name of that book, I mean, that you had your head in all yesterday?" "The Talisman, Uncle. Oh, if this should turn out to be a talisman, how enchanting it would be!" "Yes, The Talisman: ah, well, you're welcome to it, whatever it is: I must be off about my business. Is all well in the house? Does it suit you? Any complaints from the servants' hall?" "No, indeed, nothing could be more charming. The only soupçon of a complaint besides the lock of the linen closet, which I told you of, is that Mrs. Maple says she cannot get rid of the sawflies out of that room you pass through at the other end of the hall. By the way, are you sure you like your bedroom? It is a long way off from any one else, you know." "Like it? To be sure I do; the further off from you, my dear, the better. There, don't think it necessary to beat me: accept my apologies. But what are sawflies? will they eat my coats? If not, they may have the room to themselves for what I care. We are not likely to be using it." "No, of course not. Well, what she calls sawflies are those reddish things like a daddy-longlegs, but smaller,[2] and there are a great many of them perching about that room, certainly. I don't like them, but I don't fancy they are mischievous." "There seem to be several things you don't like this fine morning," said her uncle, as he closed the door. Miss Oldys remained in her chair looking at the tablet, which she was holding

[2] Apparently the ichneumon fly (Ophion obscurum), and not the true sawfly, is meant.

in the palm of her hand. The smile that had been on her face faded slowly from it and gave place to an expression of curiosity and almost strained attention. Her reverie was broken by the entrance of Mrs. Maple, and her invariable opening, "Oh, Miss, could I speak to you a minute?"

A letter from Miss Oldys to a friend in Lichfield, begun a day or two before, is the next source for this story. It is not devoid of traces of the influence of that leader of female thought in her day, Miss Anna Seward, known to some as the Swan of Lichfield.

"My sweetest Emily will be rejoiced to hear that we are at length—my beloved uncle and myself—settled in the house that now calls us master—nay, master and mistress—as in past ages it has called so many others. Here we taste a mingling of modern elegance and hoary antiquity, such as has never ere now graced life for either of us. The town, small as it is, affords us some reflection, pale indeed, but veritable, of the sweets of polite intercourse: the adjacent country numbers amid the occupants of its scattered mansions some whose polish is annually refreshed by contact with metropolitan splendour, and others whose robust and homely geniality is, at times, and by way of contrast, not less cheering and acceptable. Tired of the parlours and drawing-rooms of our friends, we have ready to hand a refuge from the clash of wits or the small talk of the day amid the solemn beauties of our venerable minster, whose silvern chimes daily 'knoll us to prayer,' and in the shady walks of whose tranquil graveyard we muse with softened heart, and ever and anon with moistened eye, upon the memorials of the young, the beautiful, the aged, the wise, and the good."

Here there is an abrupt break both in the writing and the style.

"But my dearest Emily, I can no longer write with the care which you deserve, and in which we both take pleasure. What I have to tell you is wholly foreign to what has gone before. This morning my uncle brought in to breakfast an object which had been found in the garden; it was a glass or crystal tablet of this shape (a little sketch is given), which he handed to me, and which, after he left the room, remained on the table by me. I gazed at it, I know not why, for some minutes, till called away by the day's duties; and you will smile incredulously when I say that I seemed to myself to begin to descry reflected in it objects and scenes which were not in the room where I was. You will not, however, be surprised that after such an experience I took the first opportunity to seclude myself in my room with what I now half believed to be a talisman of mickle might. I was not disappointed. I assure you, Emily, by that memory which is dearest to both of us, that what I went through this afternoon transcends the limits of what I had before deemed credible. In brief, what I saw, seated in my bedroom, in the broad daylight of summer, and looking into the crystal depth of that small round tablet, was this. First, a prospect, strange to me, of an enclosure of rough and hillocky grass, with a grey stone ruin in the midst, and a wall of rough stones about it. In this stood an old, and very ugly, woman in a red cloak and ragged skirt, talking to a boy dressed in the fashion of maybe a hundred years ago. She put something which glittered into his hand, and he something into hers, which I saw to be money, for a single coin fell from her trembling hand into the grass. The scene passed—I should have remarked, by the way, that on the rough walls of the enclosure I could distinguish bones, and even a skull, lying in a disorderly fashion. Next, I was looking upon two boys; one the figure of the former vision, the other younger. They were in a plot of garden, walled round, and this garden, in spite of the difference in arrangement, and the small size of the trees, I could clearly recognize as being that upon which I now look from my window. The boys were engaged in some curious play, it seemed. Something was smouldering on the ground. The elder placed his hands upon it, and then raised them in what I took to be an attitude of prayer: and I saw, and started at seeing, that on them were deep stains of blood. The sky above was overcast. The same boy now turned his face towards the wall of the garden, and beckoned with both his raised hands, and as he did so I was conscious that some moving objects were becoming visible over the top of the wall—whether heads or other parts of some animal or human forms I could not tell. Upon the instant the elder boy turned sharply, seized the arm of the younger (who all this time had been poring over what lay on the ground), and both hurried off. I then saw blood upon the grass, a little pile of bricks, and what I thought were black feathers scattered about. That scene closed, and the next was so dark that perhaps the full meaning of it escaped me. But what I seemed to see was a form, at first crouching low among trees or bushes that were being threshed by a violent wind, then running very swiftly, and constantly turning a pale face to look behind him, as if he feared a pursuer: and, indeed, pursuers were following hard after him. Their shapes were but dimly seen, their number—three or four, perhaps, only guessed. I suppose they were on the whole more like dogs than anything else, but dogs such as we have seen they assuredly were not. Could I have closed my eyes to this horror, I would have done so at once, but I was helpless. The last I saw was the victim darting beneath an arch and clutching at some object to which he clung: and those that were pursuing him overtook him, and I seemed to hear the echo of a cry of despair. It may be that I became unconscious: certainly I had the sensation of awaking to the light of day after an interval of darkness. Such, in literal truth, Emily, was my vision—I can call it by no other name—of this afternoon. Tell me, have I not been the unwilling witness of some episode of a tragedy connected with this very house?"

The letter is continued next day. "The tale of yesterday was not completed when I laid down my pen. I said nothing of my experiences to my uncle—you know, yourself, how little his robust common-sense would be prepared to allow of them, and how in his eyes the specific remedy would be a black draught or a glass of port. After a silent evening, then—silent, not sullen—I retired to rest. Judge of my terror, when, not yet in bed, I heard what I can only describe as a distant bellow, and knew it for my uncle's voice, though never in my hearing so exerted before. His sleeping-room is at the further extremity of this large house, and to gain access to it one must traverse an antique hall some eighty feet long and a lofty panelled chamber, and two unoccupied bedrooms. In the second of these—a room almost devoid of furniture—I found him, in the dark, his candle lying smashed on the floor. As I ran in, bearing a light, he clasped me in arms that trembled for the first time since I have known him, thanked God, and hurried me out of the room. He would say nothing of what had alarmed him. 'To-morrow, to-morrow,' was all I could get from him. A bed was hastily improvised for him in the room next to my own. I doubt if his night was more restful than mine. I could only get to sleep in the small hours, when daylight was already strong, and then my dreams were of the grimmest—particularly one which stamped itself on my brain, and which I must set down on the chance of dispersing the impression it has made. It was that I came up to my room with a heavy foreboding of evil oppressing me, and went with a hesitation and reluctance I could not explain to my chest of drawers. I opened the top drawer, in which was nothing but ribbons and handkerchiefs, and then the second, where was as little to alarm, and then, O heavens, the third and last: and there was a mass of linen neatly folded: upon which, as I looked with curiosity that began to be tinged with horror, I perceived a movement in it, and a pink hand was thrust out of the folds and began to grope feebly in the air. I could bear it no more, and rushed from the room, clapping the door after me, and strove with all my force to lock it. But the key would not turn in the wards, and from within the room came a sound of rustling and bumping, drawing nearer and nearer to the door. Why I did not flee down the stairs I know not. I continued grasping the handle, and mercifully, as the door was plucked from my hand with an irresistible force, I awoke. You may not think this very alarming, but I assure you it was so to me.

"At breakfast to-day my uncle was very uncommunicative, and I think ashamed of the fright he had given us; but afterwards he inquired of me whether Mr. Spearman was still in town, adding that he thought that was a young man who had some sense left in his head. I think you know, my dear Emily, that I am not inclined to disagree with him there, and also that I was not unlikely to be able to answer his question. To Mr. Spearman he accordingly went, and I have not seen him since. I must send this strange budget of news to you now, or it may have to wait over more than one post."

The reader will not be far out if he guesses that Miss Mary and Mr. Spearman made a match of it not very long after this month of June. Mr. Spearman was a young spark, who had a good property in the neighbourhood of Whitminster, and not unfrequently about this time spent a few days at the "King's Head," ostensibly on business. But he must have had some leisure, for his diary is copious, especially for the days of which I am telling the story. It is probable to me that he wrote this episode as fully as he could at the bidding of Miss Mary.

"Uncle Oldys (how I hope I may have the right to call him so before long!) called this morning. After throwing out a good many short remarks on indifferent topics, he said 'I wish, Spearman, you'd listen to an odd story and keep a close tongue about it just for a bit, till I get more light on it.' 'To be sure,' said I, 'you may count on me.' 'I don't know what to make of it,' he said. 'You know my bedroom. It is well away from every one else's, and I pass through the great hall and two or three other rooms to get to it.' 'Is it at the end next the minster, then?' I asked. 'Yes, it is: well, now, yesterday morning my Mary told me that the room next before it was infested with some sort of fly that the housekeeper couldn't get rid of. That may be the explanation, or it may not. What do you think?' 'Why,' said I, 'you've not yet told me what has to be explained.' 'True enough, I don't believe I have; but by-the-by, what are these sawflies? What's the size of them?' I began to wonder if he was touched in the head. 'What I call a sawfly,' I said very patiently, 'is a red animal, like a daddy-longlegs, but not so big, perhaps an inch long, perhaps less. It is very hard in the body, and to me'—I was going to say 'particularly offensive,' but he broke in, 'Come, come; an inch or less. That won't do.' 'I can only tell you,' I said, 'what I know. Would it not be better if you told me from first to last what it is that has puzzled you, and then I may be able to give you some kind of an opinion.' He gazed at me meditatively. 'Perhaps it would,' he said. 'I told Mary only to-day that I thought you had some vestiges of sense in your head.' (I bowed my acknowledgements.) 'The thing is, I've an odd kind of shyness about talking of it. Nothing of the sort has happened to me before. Well, about eleven o'clock last night, or after, I took my candle and set out for my room. I had a book in my other hand—I always read something for a few minutes before I drop off to sleep. A dangerous habit: I don't recommend it: but I know how to manage my light and my bed curtains. Now then, first, as I stepped out of my study into the great half that's next to it, and shut the door, my candle went out. I supposed I had clapped the door behind me too quick, and made a draught, and I was annoyed, for I'd no tinder-box nearer than my bedroom. But I knew my way well enough, and went on. The next thing was that my book was struck out of my hand in the dark: if I said twitched out of my hand it would better express the sensation. It fell on the floor. I picked it up, and went on, more annoyed than before, and a little startled. But as you know, that hall has many windows without curtains, and in summer nights like these it is easy to see not only where the furniture is, but whether there's any one or anything moving, and there was no one—nothing of the kind. So on I went through the hall and through the audit chamber next to it, which also has big windows, and then into the bedrooms which lead to my own, where the curtains were drawn, and I had to go slower because of steps here and there. It was in the second of those rooms that I nearly got my quietus. The moment I opened the door of it I felt there was something wrong. I thought twice, I confess, whether I shouldn't turn back and find another way there is to my room rather than go through that one. Then I was ashamed of myself, and thought what people call better of it, though I don't know about "better" in this case. If I was to describe my experience exactly, I should say this: there was a dry, light, rustling sound all over the room as I went in, and then (you remember it was perfectly dark) something seemed to rush at me, and there was—I don't know how to put it—a sensation of long thin arms, or legs, or feelers, all about my face, and neck, and body. Very little strength in them, there seemed to be, but Spearman, I don't think I was ever more horrified or disgusted in all my life, that I remember: and it does take something to put me out. I roared out as loud as I could, and flung away my candle at random, and, knowing I was near the window, I tore at the curtain and somehow let in enough light to be able to see something waving which I knew was an insect's leg, by the shape of it: but, Lord, what a size! Why the beast must have been as tall as I am. And now you tell me sawflies are an inch long or less. What do you make of it, Spearman?'

"'For goodness sake finish your story first,' I said. 'I never heard anything like it.' 'Oh,' said he, 'there's no more to tell. Mary ran in with a light, and there was nothing there. I didn't tell her what was the matter. I changed my room for last night, and I expect for good.' 'Have you searched this odd room of yours?' I said. 'What do you keep in it?' 'We don't use it,' he answered. 'There's an old press there, and some little other furniture.' 'And in the press?' said I. 'I don't know; I never saw it opened, but I do know that it's locked.' 'Well, I should have it looked into, and, if you had time, I own to having some curiosity to see the place myself.' 'I didn't exactly like to ask you, but that's rather what I hoped you'd say. Name your time and I'll take you there.' 'No time like the present,' I said at once, for I saw he would never settle down to anything while this affair was in suspense. He got up with great alacrity, and looked at me, I am tempted to think, with marked approval. 'Come along,' was all he said, however; and was pretty silent all the way to his house. My Mary (as he calls her in public, and I in private) was summoned, and we proceeded to the room. The Doctor had gone so far as to tell her that he had had something of a fright there last night, of what nature he had not yet divulged; but now he pointed out and described, very briefly, the incidents of his progress. When we were near the important spot, he pulled up, and allowed me to pass on. 'There's the room,' he said. 'Go in, Spearman, and tell us what you find.' Whatever I might have felt at midnight, noonday I was sure would keep back anything sinister, and I flung the door open with an air and stepped in. It was a well-lighted room, with its large window on the right, though not, I thought, a very airy one. The principal piece of furniture was the gaunt old press of dark wood. There was, too, a four-post bedstead, a mere skeleton which could hide nothing, and there was a chest of drawers. On the window-sill and the floor near it were the dead bodies of many hundred sawflies, and one torpid one which I had some satisfaction in killing. I tried the door of the press, but could not open it: the drawers, too, were locked. Somewhere, I was conscious, there was a faint rustling sound, but I could not locate it, and when I made my report to those outside, I said nothing of it. But, I said, clearly the next thing was to see what was in those locked receptacles. Uncle Oldys turned to

Mary. 'Mrs. Maple,' he said, and Mary ran off—no one, I am sure, steps like her—and soon came back at a soberer pace, with an elderly lady of discreet aspect.

"'Have you the keys of these things, Mrs. Maple?' said Uncle Oldys. His simple words let loose a torrent (not violent, but copious) of speech: had she been a shade or two higher in the social scale, Mrs. Maple might have stood as the model for Miss Bates.

"'Oh, Doctor, and Miss, and you too, sir,' she said, acknowledging my presence with a bend, 'them keys! who was that again that come when first we took over things in this house—a gentleman in business it was, and I gave him his luncheon in the small parlour on account of us not having everything as we should like to see it in the large one—chicken, and apple-pie, and a glass of madeira—dear, dear, you'll say I'm running on, Miss Mary; but I only mention it to bring back my recollection; and there it comes—Gardner, just the same as it did last week with the artichokes and the text of the sermon. Now that Mr. Gardner, every key I got from him were labelled to itself, and each and every one was a key of some door or another in this house, and sometimes two; and when I say door, my meaning is door of a room, not like such a press as this is. Yes, Miss Mary, I know full well, and I'm just making it clear to your uncle and you too, sir. But now there was a box which this same gentleman he give over into my charge, and thinking no harm after he was gone I took the liberty, knowing it was your uncle's property, to rattle it: and unless I'm most surprisingly deceived, in that box there was keys, but what keys, that, Doctor, is known Elsewhere, for open the box, no that I would not do.'

"I wondered that Uncle Oldys remained as quiet as he did under this address. Mary, I knew, was amused by it, and he probably had been taught by experience that it was useless to break in upon it. At any rate he did not, but merely said at the end, 'Have you that box handy, Mrs. Maple? If so, you might bring it here.' Mrs. Maple pointed her finger at him, either in accusation or in gloomy triumph. 'There,' she said, 'was I to choose out the very words out of your mouth, Doctor, them would be the ones. And if I've took it to my own rebuke one half-a-dozen times, it's been nearer fifty. Laid awake I have in my bed, sat down in my chair I have, the same you and Miss Mary gave me the day I was twenty year in your service, and no person could desire a better—yes, Miss Mary, but it is the truth, and well we know who it is would have it different if he could. "All very well," says I to myself, "but pray, when the Doctor calls you to account for that box, what are you going to say?" No, Doctor, if you was some masters I've heard of and I was some servants I could name, I should have an easy task before me, but things being, humanly speaking, what they are, the one course open to me is just to say to you that without Miss Mary comes to my room and helps me to my recollection, which her wits may manage what's slipped beyond mine, no such box as that, small though it be, will cross your eyes this many a day to come.'

"'Why, dear Mrs. Maple, why didn't you tell me before that you wanted me to help you to find it?' said my Mary. 'No, never mind telling me why it was: let us come at once and look for it.' They hastened off together. I could hear Mrs. Maple beginning an explanation which, I doubt not, lasted into the furthest recesses of the housekeeper's department. Uncle Oldys and I were left alone. 'A valuable servant,' he said, nodding towards the door. 'Nothing goes wrong under her: the speeches are seldom over three minutes.' 'How will Miss Oldys manage to make her remember about the box?' I asked.

"'Mary? Oh, she'll make her sit down and ask her about her aunt's last illness, or who gave her the china dog on the mantel-piece—something quite off the point. Then, as Maple says, one thing brings up another, and the right one will come round sooner than you could suppose. There! I believe I hear them coming back already.'

"It was indeed so, and Mrs. Maple was hurrying on ahead of Mary with the box in her outstretched hand, and a beaming face. 'What was it,' she cried as she drew near, 'what was it as I said, before ever I come out of Dorsetshire to this place? Not that I'm a Dorset woman myself, nor had need to be. "Safe bind, safe find," and there it was in the place where I'd put it—what?—two months back, I daresay.' She handed it to Uncle Oldys, and he and I examined it with some interest, so that I ceased to pay attention to Mrs. Ann Maple for the moment, though I know that she went on to expound exactly where the box had been, and in what way Mary had helped to refresh her memory on the subject.

"It was an oldish box, tied with pink tape and sealed, and on the lid was pasted a label inscribed in old ink, 'The Senior Prebendary's House, Whitminster.' On being opened it was found to contain two keys of moderate size, and a paper, on which, in the same hand as the label, was 'Keys of the Press and Box of Drawers standing in the disused Chamber.' Also this: 'The Effects in this Press and Box are held by me, and to be held by my successors in the Residence, in trust for the noble Family of Kildonan, if claim be made by any survivor of it. I having made all the Enquiry possible to myself am of the opinion that that noble House is wholly extinct: the last Earl having been, as is notorious, cast away at sea, and his only Child and Heire deceas'd in my House (the Papers as to which melancholy Casualty were by me repos'd in the same Press in this year of our Lord 1753, 21 March). I am further of opinion that unless grave discomfort arise, such persons, not being of the Family of Kildonan, as shall become possess'd of these keys, will be well advised to leave matters as they are: which opinion I do not express without weighty and sufficient reason; and am Happy to have my Judgment confirm'd by the other Members of this College and Church who are conversant with the Events referr'd to in this Paper. Tho. Ashton, S.T.P., Præb. senr. Will. Blake, S.T.P., Decanus. Hen. Goodman, S.T.B., Præb. junr.'

"'Ah!' said Uncle Oldys, 'grave discomfort! So he thought there might be something. I suspect it was that young man,' he went on, pointing with the key to the line about the 'only Child and Heire.' 'Eh, Mary? The viscounty of Kildonan was Saul.' 'How do you know that, Uncle?' said Mary. 'Oh, why not? it's all in Debrett—two little fat books. But I meant the tomb by the lime walk. He's there. What's the story, I wonder? Do you know it, Mrs. Maple? and, by the way, look at your sawflies by the window there.'

"Mrs. Maple, thus confronted with two subjects at once, was a little put to it to do justice to both. It was no doubt rash in Uncle Oldys to give her the opportunity. I could only guess that he had some slight hesitation about using the key he held in his hand.

"'Oh them flies, how bad they was, Doctor and Miss, this three or four days: and you, too, sir, you wouldn't guess, none of you! And how they come, too! First we took the room in hand, the shutters was up, and had been, I daresay, years upon years, and not a fly to be seen. Then we got the shutter bars down with a deal of trouble and left it so for the day, and next day I sent Susan in with the broom to sweep about, and not two minutes hadn't passed when out she come into the hall like a blind thing, and we had regular to beat them off her. Why her cap and her hair, you couldn't see the colour of it, I do assure you, and all clustering round her eyes, too. Fortunate enough she's not a girl with fancies, else if it had been me, why only the tickling of the nasty things would have drove me out of my wits. And now there they lay like so many dead things. Well, they was lively enough on the Monday, and now here's Thursday, is it, or no, Friday. Only to come near the door and you'd hear them pattering up against it, and once you opened it, dash at you, they would, as if they'd eat you. I couldn't help thinking to myself, "If you was bats, where should we be this night?" Nor you can't cresh 'em, not like a usual kind of a fly. Well, there's something to be thankful for, if we could but learn by it. And then this tomb, too,' she said, hastening on to her second point to elude any chance of interruption, 'of them two poor young lads. I say poor, and yet when I recollect myself, I was at tea with Mrs. Simpkins, the sexton's wife, before you come, Doctor and Miss Mary, and that's a family has been in the place, what? I daresay a hundred years in that very house, and could put their hand on any tomb or yet grave in all the yard and give you name and age. And his account of that young man, Mr. Simpkins's I mean to say—well!' She compressed her lips and nodded several times. 'Tell us, Mrs. Maple,' said Mary. 'Go on,' said Uncle Oldys. 'What about him?' said I. 'Never was such a thing seen in this place, not since Queen Mary's times and the Pope and all,' said Mrs. Maple. 'Why, do you know he lived in this very house, him and them that was with him, and for all I can tell in this identical room' (she shifted her feet uneasily on the floor). 'Who was with him? Do you mean the people of the house?' said Uncle Oldys suspiciously. 'Not to call people, Doctor, dear no,' was the answer; 'more what he brought with him from Ireland, I believe it was. No, the people in the house was the last to hear anything of his goings-on. But in the town not a family but knew how he stopped out at night: and them that was with him, why they were such as would strip the skin from the child in its grave; and a withered heart makes an ugly thin ghost, says Mr. Simpkins. But they turned on him at the last, he says, and there's the mark still to be seen on the minster door where they run him down. And that's no more than the truth, for I got him to show it to myself, and that's what he said. A lord he was, with a Bible name of a wicked king, whatever his godfathers could have been thinking of.' 'Saul was the name,' said Uncle Oldys. 'To be sure it was Saul, Doctor, and thank you; and now isn't it King Saul that we read of raising up the dead ghost that was slumbering in its tomb till he disturbed it, and isn't that a strange thing, this young lord to have such a name, and Mr. Simpkins's grandfather to see him out of his window of a dark night going about from one grave to another in the yard with a candle, and them that was with him following through the grass at his heels: and one night him to come right up to old Mr. Simpkins's window that gives on the yard and press his face up against it to find out if there was any one in the room that could see him: and only just time there was for old Mr. Simpkins to drop down like, quiet, just under the window and hold his breath, and not stir till he heard him stepping away again, and this rustling-like in the grass after him as he went, and then when he looked out of his window in the morning there was treadings in the grass and a dead man's bone. Oh, he was a cruel child for certain, but he had to pay in the end, and after.' 'After?' said Uncle Oldys, with a frown. 'Oh yes, Doctor, night after night in old Mr. Simpkins's time, and his son, that's our Mr. Simpkins's father, yes, and our own Mr. Simpkins too. Up against that same window, particular when they've had a fire of a chilly evening, with his face right on the panes, and his hands fluttering out, and his mouth open and shut, open and shut, for a minute or more, and then gone off in the dark yard. But open the window at such times, no, that they dare not do, though they could find it in their heart to pity the poor thing, that pinched up with the cold, and seemingly fading away to a nothink as the years passed on. Well, indeed, I believe it is no more than the truth what our Mr. Simpkins says on his own grandfather's word, "A withered heart makes an ugly thin ghost."' 'I daresay,' said Uncle Oldys suddenly: so suddenly that Mrs. Maple stopped short. 'Thank you. Come away, all of you.' 'Why, Uncle,' said Mary, 'are you not going to open the press after all?' Uncle Oldys blushed, actually blushed. 'My dear,' he said, 'you are at liberty to call me a coward, or applaud me as a prudent man, whichever you please. But I am neither going to open that press nor that chest of drawers myself, nor am I going to hand over the keys to you or to any other person. Mrs. Maple, will you kindly see about getting a man or two to move those pieces of furniture into the garret?' 'And when they do it, Mrs. Maple,' said Mary, who seemed to me—I did not then know why—more relieved than disappointed by her uncle's decision, 'I have something that I want put with the rest; only quite a small packet.'

"We left that curious room not unwillingly, I think. Uncle Oldys's orders were carried out that same day. And so," concludes Mr. Spearman, "Whitminster has a Bluebeard's chamber, and, I am rather inclined to suspect, a Jack-in-the-box, awaiting some future occupant of the residence of the senior prebendary."

# THE DIARY OF MR. POYNTER

The sale-room of an old and famous firm of book auctioneers in London is, of course, a great meeting-place for collectors, librarians, dealers: not only when an auction is in progress, but perhaps even more notably when books that are coming on for sale are upon view. It was in such a sale-room that the remarkable series of events began which were detailed to me not many months ago by the person whom they principally affected, namely, Mr. James Denton, M.A., F.S.A., etc., etc., some time of Trinity Hall, now, or lately, of Rendcomb Manor in the county of Warwick.

He, on a certain spring day not many years since, was in London for a few days upon business connected principally with the furnishing of the house which he had just finished building at Rendcomb. It may be a disappointment to you to learn that Rendcomb Manor was new; that I cannot help. There had, no doubt, been an old house; but it was not remarkable for beauty or interest. Even had it been, neither beauty nor interest would have enabled it to resist the disastrous fire which about a couple of years before the date of my story had razed it to the ground. I am glad to say that all that was most valuable in it had been saved, and that it was fully insured. So that it was with a comparatively light heart that Mr. Denton was able to face the task of building a new and considerably more convenient dwelling for himself and his aunt who constituted his whole ménage.

Being in London, with time on his hands, and not far from the sale-room at which I have obscurely hinted, Mr. Denton thought that he would spend an hour there upon the chance of finding, among that portion of the famous Thomas collection of MSS., which he knew to be then on view, something bearing upon the history or topography of his part of Warwickshire.

He turned in accordingly, purchased a catalogue and ascended to the sale-room, where, as usual, the books were disposed in cases and some laid out upon the long tables. At the shelves, or sitting about at the tables, were figures, many of whom were familiar to him. He exchanged nods and greetings with several, and then settled down to examine his catalogue and note likely items. He had made good progress through about two hundred of the five hundred lots—every now and then rising to take a volume from the shelf and give it a cursory glance—when a hand was laid on his shoulder, and he looked up. His interrupter was one of those intelligent men with a pointed beard and a flannel shirt, of whom the last quarter of the nineteenth century was, it seems to me, very prolific.

It is no part of my plan to repeat the whole conversation which ensued between the two. I must content myself with stating that it largely referred to common acquaintances, e.g., to the nephew of Mr. Denton's friend who had recently married and settled in Chelsea, to the sister-in-law of Mr. Denton's friend who had been seriously indisposed, but was now better, and to a piece of china which Mr. Denton's friend had purchased some months before at a price much below its true value. From which you will rightly infer that the conversation was rather in the nature of a monologue. In due time, however, the friend bethought himself that Mr. Denton was there for a purpose, and said he, "What are you looking out for in particular? I don't think there's much in this lot." "Why, I thought there might be some Warwickshire collections, but I don't see anything under Warwick in the catalogue." "No, apparently not," said the friend. "All the same, I believe I noticed something like a Warwickshire diary. What was the name again? Drayton? Potter? Painter—either a P or a D, I feel sure." He turned over the leaves quickly. "Yes, here it is. Poynter. Lot 486. That might interest you. There are the books, I think: out on the table. Some one has been looking at them. Well, I must be getting on. Good-bye, you'll look us up, won't you? Couldn't you come this afternoon? We've got a little music about four. Well, then, when you're next in town." He went off. Mr. Denton looked at his watch and found to his confusion that he could spare no more than a moment before retrieving his luggage and going for the train. The moment was just enough to show him that there were four largish volumes of the diary—that it concerned the years about 1710, and that there seemed to be a good many insertions in it of various kinds. It seemed quite worth while to leave a commission of five and twenty pounds for it, and this he was able to do, for his usual agent entered the room as he was on the point of leaving it.

That evening he rejoined his aunt at their temporary abode, which was a small dower-house not many hundred yards from the Manor. On the following morning the two resumed a discussion that had now lasted for some weeks as to the equipment of the new house. Mr. Denton laid before his relative a statement of the results of his visit to town—particulars of carpets, of chairs, of wardrobes, and of bedroom china. "Yes, dear," said his aunt, "but I don't see any chintzes here. Did you go to ----?" Mr. Denton stamped on the floor (where else, indeed, could he have stamped?). "Oh dear, oh dear," he said, "the one thing I missed. I am sorry. The fact is I was on my way there and I happened to be passing Robins's." His aunt threw up her hands. "Robins's! Then the next thing will be another parcel of horrible old books at some outrageous price. I do think, James, when I am taking all this trouble for you, you might contrive to remember the one or two things which I specially begged you to see after. It's not as if I was asking it for myself. I don't know whether you think I get any pleasure out of it, but if so I can assure you it's very much the reverse. The thought and worry and trouble I have over it you have no idea of, and you have simply to go to the shops and order the things." Mr. Denton interposed a moan of penitence. "Oh, aunt——" "Yes, that's all very well, dear, and I don't want to speak sharply, but you must know how very annoying it is: particularly as it delays the whole of our business for I can't tell how long: here is Wednesday—the Simpsons come to-morrow, and you can't leave them. Then on Saturday we have friends, as you know, coming for tennis. Yes, indeed, you spoke of asking them yourself, but, of course, I had to write the notes, and it is ridiculous, James, to look like that. We must occasionally be civil to our neighbours: you wouldn't like to have it said we were perfect bears. What was I saying? Well, anyhow it comes to this, that it must be Thursday in next week at least, before you can go to town again, and until we have decided upon the chintzes it is impossible to settle upon one single other thing."

Mr. Denton ventured to suggest that as the paint and wallpapers had been dealt with, this was too severe a view: but this his aunt was not prepared to admit at the moment. Nor, indeed, was there any proposition he could have advanced which she would have found herself able to accept. However, as the day went on, she receded a little from this position: examined with lessening disfavour the samples and price lists submitted by her nephew, and even in some cases gave a qualified approval to his choice.

As for him, he was naturally somewhat dashed by the consciousness of duty unfulfilled, but more so by the prospect of a lawn-tennis party, which, though an inevitable evil in August, he had thought there was no occasion to fear in May. But he was to some extent cheered by the arrival on the Friday morning of an intimation that he had secured at the price of £12 10s. the four volumes of Poynter's manuscript diary, and still more by the arrival on the next morning of the diary itself.

The necessity of taking Mr. and Mrs. Simpson for a drive in the car on Saturday morning and of attending to his neighbours and guests that afternoon prevented him from doing more than open the parcel until the party had retired to bed on the Saturday night. It was then that he made certain of the fact, which he had before only suspected, that he had indeed acquired the diary of Mr. William Poynter, Squire of Acrington (about four miles from his own parish)—that same Poynter who was for a time a member of the circle of Oxford antiquaries, the centre of which was Thomas Hearne, and with whom Hearne seems ultimately to have quarrelled—a not uncommon episode in the career of that excellent man. As is the case with Hearne's own collections, the diary of Poynter contained a good many notes from printed books, descriptions of coins and other antiquities that had been brought to his notice, and drafts of letters on these subjects, besides the chronicle of everyday events. The description in the sale-catalogue had given Mr. Denton no idea of the amount of interest which seemed to lie in the book, and he sat up reading in the first of the four volumes until a reprehensibly late hour.

On the Sunday morning, after church, his aunt came into the study and was diverted from what she had been going to say to him by the sight of the four brown leather quartos on the table. "What are these?" she said suspiciously. "New, aren't they? Oh! are these the things that made you forget my chintzes? I thought so. Disgusting. What did you give for them, I should like to know? Over Ten Pounds? James, it is really sinful. Well, if you have money to throw away on this kind of thing, there can be no reason why you should not subscribe—and subscribe handsomely—to my anti-Vivisection League. There is not, indeed, James, and I shall be very seriously annoyed if——. Who did you say wrote them? Old Mr. Poynter, of Acrington? Well, of course, there is some interest in getting together old papers about this neighbourhood. But Ten Pounds!" She picked up one of the volumes—not that which her nephew had been reading—and opened it at random, dashing it to the floor the next instant with a cry of disgust as a earwig fell from between the pages. Mr. Denton picked it up with a smothered expletive and said, "Poor book! I think you're rather hard on Mr. Poynter." "Was I, my dear? I beg his pardon, but you know I cannot abide those horrid creatures. Let me see if I've done any mischief." "No, I think all's well: but look here what you've opened him on." "Dear me, yes, to be sure! how very interesting. Do unpin it, James, and let me look at it."

It was a piece of patterned stuff about the size of the quarto page, to which it was fastened by an old-fashioned pin. James detached it and handed it to his aunt, carefully replacing the pin in the paper.

Now, I do not know exactly what the fabric was; but it had a design printed upon it, which completely fascinated Miss Denton. She went into raptures over it, held it against the wall, made James do the same, that she might retire to contemplate it from a distance: then pored over it at close quarters, and ended her examination by expressing in the warmest terms her appreciation of the taste of the ancient Mr. Poynter who had had the happy idea of preserving this sample in his diary. "It is a most charming pattern," she said, "and remarkable too. Look, James, how delightfully the lines ripple. It reminds one of hair, very much, doesn't it. And then these knots of ribbon at intervals. They give just the relief of colour that is wanted. I wonder——" "I was going to say," said James with deference, "I wonder if it would cost much to have it copied for our curtains." "Copied? how could you have it copied, James?" "Well, I don't know the details, but I suppose that is a printed pattern, and that you could have a block cut from it in wood or metal." "Now, really, that is a capital idea, James. I am almost inclined to be glad that you were so—that you forgot the chintzes on Monday. At any rate, I'll promise to forgive and forget if you get this lovely old thing copied. No one will have anything in the least like it, and mind, James, we won't allow it to be sold. Now I must go, and I've totally forgotten what it was I came in to say: never mind, it'll keep."

After his aunt had gone James Denton devoted a few minutes to examining the pattern more closely than he had yet had a chance of doing. He was puzzled to think why it should have struck Miss Benton so forcibly. It seemed to him not specially remarkable or pretty. No doubt it was suitable enough for a curtain pattern: it ran in vertical bands, and there was some indication that these were intended to converge at the top. She was right, too, in thinking that these main bands resembled rippling—almost curling—tresses of hair. Well, the main thing was to find out by means of trade directories, or otherwise, what firm would undertake the reproduction of an old pattern of this kind. Not to delay the reader over this portion of the story, a list of likely names was made out, and Mr. Denton fixed a day for calling on them, or some of them, with his sample.

The first two visits which he paid were unsuccessful: but there is luck in odd numbers. The firm in Bermondsey which was third on his list was accustomed to handling this line. The evidence they were able to produce justified their being entrusted with the job. "Our Mr. Cattell" took a fervent personal interest in it. "It's 'eartrending, isn't it, sir," he said, "to picture the quantity of reelly lovely medeevial stuff of this kind that lays well-nigh unnoticed in many of our residential country 'ouses: much of it in peril, I take it, of being cast aside as so much rubbish. What is it Shakespeare says—unconsidered trifles. Ah, I often say he 'as a word for us all, sir. I say Shakespeare, but I'm well aware all don't 'old with me there—I 'ad something of an upset the other day when a gentleman came in—a titled man, too, he was, and I think he told me he'd wrote on the topic, and I 'appened to cite out something about 'Ercules and the painted cloth. Dear me, you never see such a pother. But as to this, what you've kindly confided to us, it's a piece of work we shall take a reel enthusiasm in achieving it out to the very best of our ability. What man 'as done, as I was observing only a few weeks back to another esteemed client, man can do, and in three to four weeks' time, all being well, we shall 'ope to lay before you evidence to that effect, sir. Take the address, Mr. 'Iggins, if you please."

Such was the general drift of Mr. Cattell's observations on the occasion of his first interview with Mr. Denton. About a month later, being advised that some samples were ready for his inspection, Mr. Denton met him again, and had, it seems, reason to be satisfied with the faithfulness of the reproduction of the design. It had been finished off at the top in accordance with the indication I mentioned, so that the vertical bands joined. But something still needed to be done in the way of matching the colour of the original. Mr. Cattell had suggestions of a technical kind to offer, with which I need not trouble you. He had also views as to the general desirability of the pattern which were vaguely adverse. "You say you don't wish this to be supplied excepting to personal friends equipped with a authorization from yourself, sir. It shall be done. I quite understand your wish to keep it exclusive: lends it a catchit, does it not, to the suite? What's every man's, it's been said, is no man's."

"Do you think it would be popular if it were generally obtainable?" asked Mr. Denton.

"I 'ardly think it, sir," said Cattell, pensively clasping his beard. "I 'ardly think it. Not popular: it wasn't popular with the man that cut the block, was it, Mr. 'Iggins?"

"Did he find it a difficult job?"

"He'd no call to do so, sir; but the fact is that the artistic temperament—and our men are artists, sir, every man of them—true artists as much as many that the world styles by that term—it's apt to take some strange 'ardly accountable likes or dislikes, and here was an example. The twice or thrice that I went to inspect his progress: language I could understand, for that's 'abitual to him, but reel distaste for what I should call a dainty enough thing, I did not, nor am I now able to fathom. It seemed," said Mr. Cattell, looking narrowly upon Mr. Denton, "as if the man scented something almost Hevil in the design."

"Indeed? did he tell you so? I can't say I see anything sinister in it myself."

"Neether can I, sir. In fact I said as much. 'Come, Gatwick,' I said, 'what's to do here? What's the reason of your prejudice—for I can call it no more than that?' But, no! no explanation was forthcoming. And I was merely reduced, as I am now, to a shrug of the shoulders, and a cui bono. However, here it is," and with that the technical side of the question came to the front again.

The matching of the colours for the background, the hem, and the knots of ribbon was by far the longest part of the business, and necessitated many sendings to and fro of the original pattern and of new samples. During part of August and September, too, the Dentons were away from the Manor. So that it was not until October was well in that a sufficient quantity of the stuff had been manufactured to furnish curtains for the three or four bedrooms which were to be fitted up with it.

On the feast of Simon and Jude the aunt and nephew returned from a short visit to find all completed, and their satisfaction at the general effect was great. The new curtains, in particular, agreed to admiration with their surroundings. When Mr. Denton was dressing for dinner, and took stock of his room, in which there was a large amount of the chintz displayed, he congratulated himself over and over again on the luck which had first made him forget his aunt's commission and had then put into his hands this extremely effective means of remedying his mistake. The pattern was, as he said at dinner, so restful and yet so far from being dull. And Miss Denton—

who, by the way, had none of the stuff in her own room—was much disposed to agree with him.

At breakfast next morning he was induced to qualify his satisfaction to some extent—but very slightly. "There is one thing I rather regret," he said, "that we allowed them to join up the vertical bands of the pattern at the top. I think it would have been better to leave that alone."

"Oh?" said his aunt interrogatively.

"Yes: as I was reading in bed last night they kept catching my eye rather. That is, I found myself looking across at them every now and then. There was an effect as if some one kept peeping out between the curtains in one place or another, where there was no edge, and I think that was due to the joining up of the bands at the top. The only other thing that troubled me was the wind."

"Why, I thought it was a perfectly still night."

"Perhaps it was only on my side of the house, but there was enough to sway my curtains and rustle them more than I wanted."

That night a bachelor friend of James Denton's came to stay, and was lodged in a room on the same floor as his host, but at the end of a long passage, halfway down which was a red baize door, put there to cut off the draught and intercept noise.

The party of three had separated. Miss Denton a good first, the two men at about eleven. James Denton, not yet inclined for bed, sat him down in an arm-chair and read for a time. Then he dozed, and then he woke, and bethought himself that his brown spaniel, which ordinarily slept in his room, had not come upstairs with him. Then he thought he was mistaken: for happening to move his hand which hung down over the arm of the chair within a few inches of the floor, he felt on the back of it just the slightest touch of a surface of hair, and stretching it out in that direction he stroked and patted a rounded something. But the feel of it, and still more the fact that instead of a responsive movement, absolute stillness greeted his touch, made him look over the arm. What he had been touching rose to meet him. It was in the attitude of one that had crept along the floor on its belly, and it was, so far as could be collected, a human figure. But of the face which was now rising to within a few inches of his own no feature was discernible, only hair. Shapeless as it was, there was about it so horrible an air of menace that as he bounded from his chair and rushed from the room he heard himself moaning with fear: and doubtless he did right to fly. As he dashed into the baize door that cut the passage in two, and—forgetting that it opened towards him—beat against it with all the force in him, he felt a soft ineffectual tearing at his back which, all the same, seemed to be growing in power, as if the hand, or whatever worse than a hand was there, were becoming more material as the pursuer's rage was more concentrated. Then he remembered the trick of the door—he got it open—he shut it behind him—he gained his friend's room, and that is all we need know.

It seems curious that, during all the time that had elapsed since the purchase of Poynter's diary, James Denton should not have sought an explanation of the presence of the pattern that had been pinned into it. Well, he had read the diary through without finding it mentioned, and had concluded that there was nothing to be said. But, on leaving Rendcomb Manor (he did not know whether for good), as he naturally insisted upon doing on the day after experiencing the horror I have tried to put into words, he took the diary with him. And at his seaside lodgings he examined more narrowly the portion whence the pattern had been taken. What he remembered having suspected about it turned out to be correct. Two or three leaves were pasted together, but written upon, as was patent when they were held up to the light. They yielded easily to steaming, for the paste had lost much of its strength, and they contained something relevant to the pattern.

The entry was made in 1707.

> *"Old Mr. Casbury, of Acrington, told me this day much of young Sir Everard Charlett, whom he remember'd Commoner of University College, and thought was of the same Family as Dr. Arthur Charlett, now master of ye Coll. This Charlett was a personable young gent., but a loose atheistical companion, and a great Lifter, as they then call'd the hard drinkers, and for what I know do so now. He was noted, and subject to severall censures at different times for his extravagancies: and if the full history of his debaucheries had bin known, no doubt would have been expell'd ye Coll., supposing that no interest had been imploy'd on his behalf, of which Mr. Casbury had some suspicion. He was a very beautiful person, and constantly wore his own Hair, which was*

*very abundant, from which, and his loose way of living, the cant name for him was Absalom, and he was accustom'd to say that indeed he believ'd he had shortened old David's days, meaning his father, Sir Job Charlett, an old worthy cavalier.*

*"Note that Mr. Casbury said that he remembers not the year of Sir Everard Charlett's death, but it was 1692 or 3. He died suddenly in October. [Several lines describing his unpleasant habits and reputed delinquencies are omitted.] Having seen him in such topping spirits the night before, Mr. Casbury was amaz'd when he learn'd the death. He was found in the town ditch, the hair as was said pluck'd clean off his head. Most bells in Oxford rung out for him, being a nobleman, and he was buried next night in St. Peter's in the East. But two years after, being to be moved to his country estate by his successor, it was said the coffin, breaking by mischance, proved quite full of Hair: which sounds fabulous, but yet I believe precedents are upon record, as in Dr. Plot's History of Staffordshire.*

*"His chambers being afterwards stripp'd, Mr. Casbury came by part of the hangings of it, which 'twas said this Charlett had design'd expressly for a memorial of his Hair, giving the Fellow that drew it a lock to work by, and the piece which I have fasten'd in here was parcel of the same, which Mr. Casbury gave to me. He said he believ'd there was a subtlety in the drawing, but had never discover'd it himself, nor much liked to pore upon it."*

The money spent upon the curtains might as well have been thrown into the fire, as they were. Mr. Cattell's comment upon what he heard of the story took the form of a quotation from Shakespeare. You may guess it without difficulty. It began with the words "There are more things."

# AN EPISODE OF CATHEDRAL HISTORY

There was once a learned gentleman who was deputed to examine and report upon the archives of the Cathedral of Southminster. The examination of these records demanded a very considerable expenditure of time: hence it became advisable for him to engage lodgings in the city: for though the Cathedral body were profuse in their offers of hospitality, Mr. Lake felt that he would prefer to be master of his day. This was recognized as reasonable. The Dean eventually wrote advising Mr. Lake, if he were not already suited, to communicate with Mr. Worby, the principal Verger, who occupied a house convenient to the church and was prepared to take in a quiet lodger for three or four weeks. Such an arrangement was precisely what Mr. Lake desired. Terms were easily agreed upon, and early in December, like another Mr. Datchery (as he remarked to himself), the investigator found himself in the occupation of a very comfortable room in an ancient and "cathedraly" house.

One so familiar with the customs of Cathedral churches, and treated with such obvious consideration by the Dean and Chapter of this Cathedral in particular, could not fail to command the respect of the Head Verger. Mr. Worby even acquiesced in certain modifications of statements he had been accustomed to offer for years to parties of visitors. Mr. Lake, on his part, found the Verger a very cheery companion, and took advantage of any occasion that presented itself for enjoying his conversation when the day's work was over.

One evening, about nine o'clock, Mr. Worby knocked at his lodger's door. "I've occasion," he said, "to go across to the Cathedral, Mr. Lake, and I think I made you a promise when I did so next I would give you the opportunity to see what it looks like at night time. It is quite fine and dry outside, if you care to come."

"To be sure I will; very much obliged to you, Mr. Worby, for thinking of it, but let me get my coat."

"Here it is, sir, and I've another lantern here that you'll find advisable for the steps, as there's no moon."

"Any one might think we were Jasper and Durdles, over again, mightn't they," said Lake, as they crossed the close, for he had ascertained that the Verger had read Edwin Drood.

"Well, so they might," said Mr. Worby, with a short laugh, "though I don't know whether we ought to take it as a compliment. Odd ways, I often think, they had at that Cathedral, don't it seem so to you, sir? Full choral matins at seven o'clock in the morning all the year round. Wouldn't suit our boys' voices nowadays, and I think there's one or two of the men would be applying for a rise if the Chapter was to bring it in—particular the alltoes."

They were now at the south-west door. As Mr. Worby was unlocking it, Lake said, "Did you ever find anybody locked in here by accident?"

"Twice I did. One was a drunk sailor; however he got in I don't know. I s'pose he went to sleep in the service, but by the time I got to him he was praying fit to bring the roof in. Lor'! what a noise that man did make! said it was the first time he'd been inside a church for ten years, and blest if ever he'd try it again. The other was an old sheep: them boys it was, up to their games. That was the last time they tried it on, though. There, sir, now you see what we look like; our late Dean used now and again to bring parties in, but he preferred a moonlight night, and there was a piece of verse he'd coat to 'em, relating to a Scotch cathedral, I understand; but I don't know; I almost think the effect's better when it's all dark-like. Seems to add to the size and heighth. Now if you won't mind stopping somewhere in the nave while I go up into the choir where my business lays, you'll see what I mean."

Accordingly Lake waited, leaning against a pillar, and watched the light wavering along the length of the church, and up the steps into the choir, until it was intercepted by some screen or other furniture, which only allowed the reflection to be seen on the piers and roof. Not many minutes had passed before Worby reappeared at the door of the choir and by waving his lantern signalled to Lake to rejoin him.

"I suppose it is Worby, and not a substitute," thought Lake to himself, as he walked up the nave. There was, in fact, nothing untoward. Worby showed him the papers which he had come to fetch out of the Dean's stall, and asked him what he thought of the spectacle: Lake agreed that it was well worth seeing. "I suppose," he said, as they walked towards the altar-steps together, "that you're too much used to going about here at night to feel nervous—but you must get a start every now and then, don't you, when a book falls down or a door swings to."

"No, Mr. Lake, I can't say I think much about noises, not nowadays: I'm much more afraid of finding an escape of gas or a burst in the stove pipes than anything else. Still there have been times, years ago. Did you notice that plain altar-tomb there—fifteenth century we say it is, I don't know if you agree to that? Well, if you didn't look at it, just come back and give it a glance, if you'd be so good." It was on the north side of the choir, and rather awkwardly placed: only about three feet from the enclosing stone screen. Quite plain, as the Verger had said, but for some ordinary stone panelling. A metal cross of some size on the northern side (that next to the screen) was the solitary feature of any interest.

Lake agreed that it was not earlier than the Perpendicular period: "but," he said, "unless it's the tomb of some remarkable person, you'll forgive me for saying that I don't think it's particularly noteworthy."

"Well, I can't say as it is the tomb of anybody noted in 'istory," said Worby, who had a dry smile on his face, "for we don't own any record whatsoever of who it was put up to. For all that, if you've half an hour to spare, sir, when we get back to the house, Mr. Lake, I could tell you a tale about that tomb. I won't begin on it now; it strikes cold here, and we don't want to be dawdling about all night."

"Of course I should like to hear it immensely."

"Very well, sir, you shall. Now if I might put a question to you," he went on, as they passed down the choir aisle, "in our little local guide—and not only there, but in the little book on our Cathedral in the series—you'll find it stated that this portion of the building was erected previous to the twelfth century. Now of course I should be glad enough to take that view, but—mind the step, sir—but, I put it to you—does the lay of the stone 'ere in this portion of the wall (which he tapped with his key) does it to your eye carry the flavour of what you might call Saxon masonry? No? I thought not; no more it does to me: now, if you'll believe me, I've said as much to those men—one's the librarian of our Free Libry here, and the other came down from London on purpose—fifty times, if I have once, but I might just as well have talked to that bit of stonework. But there it is, I suppose every one's got their opinions."

The discussion of this peculiar trait of human nature occupied Mr.

Worby almost up to the moment when he and Lake re-entered the former's house. The condition of the fire in Lake's sitting-room led to a suggestion from Mr. Worby that they should finish the evening in his own parlour. We find them accordingly settled there some short time afterwards.

Mr. Worby made his story a long one, and I will not undertake to tell it wholly in his own words, or in his own order. Lake committed the substance of it to paper immediately after hearing it, together with some few passages of the narrative which had fixed themselves verbatim in his mind; I shall probably find it expedient to condense Lake's record to some extent.

Mr. Worby was born, it appeared, about the year 1828. His father before him had been connected with the Cathedral, and likewise his grandfather. One or both had been choristers, and in later life both had done work as mason and carpenter respectively about the fabric. Worby himself, though possessed, as he frankly acknowledged, of an indifferent voice, had been drafted into the choir at about ten years of age.

It was in 1840 that the wave of the Gothic revival smote the Cathedral of Southminster. "There was a lot of lovely stuff went then, sir," said Worby, with a sigh. "My father couldn't hardly believe it when he got his orders to clear out the choir. There was a new dean just come in—Dean Burscough it was—and my father had been 'prenticed to a good firm of joiners in the city, and knew what good work was when he saw it. Crool it was, he used to say: all that beautiful wainscot oak, as good as the day it was put up, and garlands-like of foliage and fruit, and lovely old gilding work on the coats of arms and the organ pipes. All went to the timber yard—every bit except some little pieces worked up in the Lady Chapel, and 'ere in this overmantel. Well—I may be mistook, but I say our choir never looked as well since. Still there was a lot found out about the history of the church, and no doubt but what it did stand in need of repair. There were very few winters passed but what we'd lose a pinnicle." Mr. Lake expressed his concurrence with Worby's views of restoration, but owns to a fear about this point lest the story proper should never be reached. Possibly this was perceptible in his manner.

Worby hastened to reassure him, "Not but what I could carry on about that topic for hours at a time, and do do when I see my opportunity. But Dean Burscough he was very set on the Gothic period, and nothing would serve him but everything must be made agreeable to that. And one morning after service he appointed for my father to meet him in the choir, and he came back after he'd taken off his robes in the vestry, and he'd got a roll of paper with him, and the verger that was then brought in a table, and they begun spreading it out on the table with prayer books to keep it down, and my father helped 'em, and he saw it was a picture of the inside of a choir in a Cathedral; and the Dean—he was a quick spoken gentleman—he says, 'Well, Worby, what do you think of that?' 'Why', says my father, 'I don't think I 'ave the pleasure of knowing that view. Would that be Hereford Cathedral, Mr. Dean?' 'No, Worby,' says the Dean, 'that's Southminster Cathedral as we hope to see it before many years.' 'In-deed, sir,' says my father, and that was all he did say—leastways to the Dean—but he used to tell me he felt really faint in himself when he looked round our choir as I can remember it, all comfortable and furnished-like, and then see this nasty little dry picter, as he called it, drawn out by some London architect. Well, there I am again. But you'll see what I mean if you look at this old view."

Worby reached down a framed print from the wall. "Well, the long and the short of it was that the Dean he handed over to my father a copy of an order of the Chapter that he was to clear out every bit of the choir—make a clean sweep—ready for the new work that was being designed up in town, and he was to put it in hand as soon as ever he could get the breakers together. Now then, sir, if you look at that view, you'll see where the pulpit used to stand: that's what I want you to notice, if you please." It was, indeed, easily seen; an unusually large structure of timber with a domed sounding-board, standing at the east end of the stalls on the north side of the choir, facing the bishop's throne. Worby proceeded to explain that during the alterations, services were held in the nave, the members of the choir being thereby disappointed of an anticipated holiday, and the organist in particular incurring the suspicion of having wilfully damaged the mechanism of the temporary organ that was hired at considerable expense from London.

The work of demolition began with the choir screen and organ loft, and proceeded gradually eastwards, disclosing, as Worby said, many interesting features of older work. While this was going on, the members of the Chapter were, naturally, in and about the choir a great deal, and it soon became apparent to the elder Worby—who could not help overhearing some of their talk—that, on the part of the senior Canons especially, there must have been a good deal of disagreement before the policy now being carried out had been adopted. Some were of opinion that they should catch their deaths of cold in the return-stalls, unprotected by a screen from the draughts in the nave: others objected to being exposed to the view of persons in the choir aisles, especially, they said, during the sermons, when they found it helpful to listen in a posture which was liable to misconstruction. The strongest opposition, however, came from the oldest of the body, who up to the last moment objected to the removal of the pulpit. "You ought not to touch it, Mr. Dean," he said with great emphasis one morning, when the two were standing before it: "you don't know what mischief you may do." "Mischief? it's not a work of any particular merit, Canon." "Don't call me Canon," said the old man with great asperity, "that is, for thirty years I've been known as Dr. Ayloff, and I shall be obliged, Mr. Dean, if you would kindly humour me in that matter. And as to the pulpit (which I've preached from for thirty years, though I don't insist on that) all I'll say is, I know you're doing wrong in moving it." "But what sense could there be, my dear Doctor, in leaving it where it is, when we're fitting up the rest of the choir in a totally different style? What reason could be given—apart from the look of the thing?" "Reason! reason!" said old Dr. Ayloff; "if you young men—if I may say so without any disrespect, Mr. Dean—if you'd only listen to reason a little, and not be always asking for it, we should get on better. But there, I've said my say." The old gentleman hobbled off, and as it proved, never entered the Cathedral again. The season—it was a hot summer—turned sickly on a sudden. Dr. Ayloff was one of the first to go, with some affection of the muscles of the thorax, which took him painfully at night. And at many services the number of choirmen and boys was very thin.

Meanwhile the pulpit had been done away with. In fact, the sounding-board (part of which still exists as a table in a summer-house in the palace garden) was taken down within an hour or two of Dr. Ayloff's protest. The removal of the base—not effected without considerable trouble—disclosed to view, greatly to the exultation of the restoring party, an altar-tomb—the tomb, of course, to which Worby had attracted Lake's attention that same evening. Much fruitless research was expended in attempts to identify the occupant; from that day to this he has never had a name put to him. The structure had been most carefully boxed in under the pulpit-base, so that such slight ornament as it possessed was not defaced; only on the north side of it there was what looked like an injury; a gap between two of the slabs composing the side. It might be two or three inches across. Palmer, the mason, was directed to fill it up in a week's time, when he came to do some other small jobs near that part of the choir.

The season was undoubtedly a very trying one. Whether the church was built on a site that had once been a marsh, as was suggested, or for whatever reason, the residents in its immediate neighbourhood had, many of them, but little enjoyment of the exquisite sunny days and the calm nights of August and September. To several of the older people—Dr. Ayloff, among others, as we have seen—the summer proved downright fatal, but even among the younger, few escaped either a sojourn in bed for a matter of weeks, or at the least, a brooding sense of oppression, accompanied by hateful nightmares. Gradually there formulated itself a suspicion—which grew into a conviction—that the alterations in the Cathedral had something to say in the matter. The widow of a former old verger, a pensioner of the Chapter of Southminster, was visited by dreams, which she retailed to her friends, of a shape that slipped out of the little door of the south transept as the dark fell in, and flitted—taking a fresh direction every night—about the close, disappearing for a while in house after house, and finally emerging again when the night sky was paling. She could see nothing of it, she said, but that it was a moving form: only she had an impression that when it returned to the church, as it seemed to do in the end of the dream, it turned its head: and then, she could not tell why, but she thought it had red eyes. Worby remembered hearing the old lady tell this dream at a tea-party in the house of the chapter clerk. Its recurrence might, perhaps, he said, be taken as a symptom of approaching illness; at any rate before the end of September the old lady was in her grave.

The interest excited by the restoration of this great church was not confined to its own county. One day that summer an F.S.A., of some celebrity, visited the place. His business was to write an account of the discoveries that had been made, for the Society of Antiquaries, and his wife, who accompanied him, was to make a series of illustrative drawings for his report. In the morning she employed herself in making a general sketch of the choir; in the afternoon she devoted herself to details. She first drew the newly exposed altar-tomb, and when that was finished, she called her husband's attention to a beautiful piece of diaper-ornament on the screen just behind it, which had, like the tomb itself, been completely concealed by the pulpit. Of course, he said, an illustration of that must be made; so she seated herself on the tomb and began a careful drawing which occupied her till dusk.

Her husband had by this time finished his work of measuring and description, and they agreed that it was time to be getting back to their hotel. "You may as well brush my skirt, Frank," said the lady, "it must have got covered with dust, I'm sure." He obeyed dutifully; but, after a moment, he said, "I don't know whether you value this dress particularly, my dear, but I'm inclined to think it's seen its best days. There's a great bit of it gone." "Gone? Where?" said she. "I don't know where it's gone, but it's off at the bottom edge behind here." She pulled it hastily into sight, and was horrified to find a jagged tear extending some way into the substance of the stuff; very much, she said, as if a dog had rent it away. The dress was, in any case, hopelessly spoilt, to her great vexation, and though they looked everywhere, the missing piece could not be found. There were many ways, they concluded, in which the injury might have come about, for the choir was full of old bits of woodwork with nails sticking out of them. Finally, they could only suppose that one of these had caused the mischief, and that the workmen, who had been about all day, had carried off the particular piece with the fragment of dress still attached to it.

It was about this time, Worby thought, that his little dog began to wear an anxious expression when the hour for it to be put into the shed in the back yard approached. (For his mother had ordained that it must not sleep in the house.) One evening, he said, when he was just going to pick it up and carry it out, it looked at him "like a Christian, and waved its 'and, I was going to say—well, you know 'ow they do carry on sometimes, and the end of it was I put it under my coat, and 'uddled it upstairs—and I'm afraid I as good as deceived my poor mother on the subject. After that the dog acted very artful with 'iding itself under the bed for half-an-hour or more before bed-time came, and we worked it so as my mother never found out what we'd done." Of course Worby was glad of its company anyhow, but more particularly when the nuisance that is still remembered in Southminster as "the crying" set in.

"Night after night," said Worby, "that dog seemed to know it was coming; he'd creep out, he would, and snuggle into the bed and cuddle right up to me shivering, and when the crying come he'd be like a wild thing, shoving his head under my arm, and I was fully near as bad. Six or seven times we'd hear it, not more, and when he'd dror out his 'ed again I'd know it was over for that night. What was it like, sir? Well, I never heard but one thing that seemed to hit it off. I happened to be playing about in the Close, and there was two of the Canons met and said 'Good morning' one to another.

'Sleep well last night?' says one—it was Mr. Henslow that one, and Mr. Lyall was the other—'Can't say I did,' says Mr. Lyall, 'rather too much of Isaiah 34. 14 for me.' '34. 14,' says Mr. Henslow, 'what's that?' 'You call yourself a Bible reader!' says Mr. Lyall. (Mr. Henslow, you must know, he was one of what used to be termed Simeon's lot—pretty much what we should call the Evangelical party.) 'You go and look it up.' I wanted to know what he was getting at myself, and so off I ran home and got out my own Bible, and there it was: 'the satyr shall cry to his fellow.' Well, I thought, is that what we've been listening to these past nights? and I tell you it made me look over my shoulder a time or two. Of course I'd asked my father and mother about what it could be before that, but they both said it was most likely cats: but they spoke very short, and I could see they was troubled. My word! that was a noise—'ungry-like, as if it was calling after some one that wouldn't come. If ever you felt you wanted company, it would be when you was waiting for it to begin again. I believe two or three nights there was men put on to watch in different parts of the Close; but they all used to get together in one corner, the nearest they could to the High Street, and nothing came of it.

"Well, the next thing was this. Me and another of the boys—he's in business in the city now as a grocer, like his father before him—we'd gone up in the Close after morning service was over, and we heard old Palmer the mason bellowing to some of his men. So we went up nearer, because we knew he was a rusty old chap and there might be some fun going. It appears Palmer'd told this man to stop up the chink in that old tomb. Well, there was this man keeping on saying he'd done it the best he could, and there was Palmer carrying on like all possessed about it. 'Call that making a job of it?' he says. 'If you had your rights you'd get the sack for this. What do you suppose I pay you your wages for? What do you suppose I'm going to say to the Dean and Chapter when they come round, as come they may do any time, and see where you've been bungling about covering the 'ole place with mess and plaster and Lord knows what?' 'Well, master, I done the best I could,' says the man; 'I don't know no more than what you do 'ow it come to fall out this way. I tamped it right in the 'ole,' he says, 'and now it's fell out,' he says, 'I never see.'

"'Fell out?' says old Palmer, 'why it's nowhere near the place. Blowed out, you mean,' and he picked up a bit of plaster, and so did I, that was laying up against the screen, three or four feet off, and not dry yet; and old Palmer he looked at it curious-like, and then he turned round on me and he says, 'Now then, you boys, have you been up to some of your games here?' 'No,' I says, 'I haven't, Mr. Palmer; there's none of us been about here till just this minute,' and while I was talking the other boy, Evans, he got looking in through the chink, and I heard him draw in his breath, and he came away sharp and up to us, and says he, 'I believe there's something in there. I saw something shiny.' 'What! I daresay,' says old Palmer; 'Well, I ain't got time to stop about there. You, William, you go off and get some more stuff and make a job of it this time; if not, there'll be trouble in my yard,' he says.

"So the man he went off, and Palmer too, and us boys stopped behind, and I says to Evans, 'Did you really see anything in there?' 'Yes,' he says, 'I did indeed.' So then I says, 'Let's shove something in and stir it up.' And we tried several of the bits of wood that was laying about, but they were all too big. Then Evans he had a sheet of music he'd brought with him, an anthem or a service, I forget which it was now, and he rolled it up small and shoved it in the chink; two or three times he did it, and nothing happened. 'Give it me, boy,' I said, and I had a try. No, nothing happened. Then, I don't know why I thought of it, I'm sure, but I stooped down just opposite the chink and put my two fingers in my mouth and whistled—you know the way—and at that I seemed to think I heard something stirring, and I says to Evans, 'Come away,' I says; 'I don't like this.' 'Oh, rot,' he says, 'Give me that roll,' and he took it and shoved it in. And I don't think ever I see any one go so pale as he did. 'I say, Worby,' he says, 'it's caught, or else some one's got hold of it.' 'Pull it out or leave it,' I says, 'Come and let's get off.' So he gave a good pull, and it came away. Leastways most of it did, but the end was gone. Torn off it was, and Evans looked at it for a second and then he gave a sort of a croak and let it drop, and we both made off out of there as quick as ever we could. When we got outside Evans says to me, 'Did you see the end of that paper.' 'No,' I says, 'only it was torn.' 'Yes, it was,' he says, 'but it was wet too, and black!' Well, partly because of the fright we had, and partly because that music was wanted in a day or two, and we knew there'd be a set-out about it with the organist, we didn't say nothing to any one else, and I suppose the workmen they swept up the bit that was left along with the rest of the rubbish. But Evans, if you were to ask him this very day about it, he'd stick to it he saw that paper wet and black at the end where it was torn."

After that the boys gave the choir a wide berth, so that Worby was not sure what was the result of the mason's renewed mending of the tomb. Only he made out from fragments of conversation dropped by the workmen passing through the choir that some difficulty had been met with, and that the governor—Mr. Palmer to wit—had tried his own hand at the job. A little later, he happened to see Mr. Palmer himself knocking at the door of the Deanery and being admitted by the butler. A day or so after that, he gathered from a remark his father let fall at breakfast that something a little out of the common was to be done in the Cathedral after morning service on the morrow. "And I'd just as soon it was to-day," his father added, "I don't see the use of running risks." "'Father,' I says, 'what are you going to do in the Cathedral to-morrow?' and he turned on me as savage as I ever see him—he was a wonderful good-tempered man as a general thing, my poor father was. 'My lad,' he says, 'I'll trouble you not to go picking up your elders' and betters' talk: it's not manners and it's not straight. What I'm going to do or not going to do in the Cathedral to-morrow is none of your business: and if I catch sight of you hanging about the place to-morrow after your work's done, I'll send you home with a flea in your ear. Now you mind that.' Of course I said I was very sorry and that, and equally of course I went off and laid my plans with Evans. We knew there was a stair up in the corner of the transept which you can get up to the triforium, and in them days the door to it was pretty well always open, and even if it wasn't we knew the key usually laid under a bit of matting hard by. So we made up our minds we'd be putting away music and that, next morning while the rest of the boys was clearing off, and then slip up the stairs and watch from the triforium if there was any signs of work going on.

"Well, that same night I dropped off asleep as sound as a boy does, and all of a sudden the dog woke me up, coming into the bed, and thought I, now we're going to get it sharp, for he seemed more frightened than usual. After about five minutes sure enough came this cry. I can't give you no idea what it was like; and so near too—nearer than I'd heard it yet—and a funny thing, Mr. Lake, you know what a place this Close is for an echo, and particular if you stand this side of it. Well, this crying never made no sign of an echo at all. But, as I said, it was dreadful near this night; and on the top of the start I got with hearing it, I got another fright; for I heard something rustling outside in the passage. Now to be sure I thought I was done; but I noticed the dog seemed to perk up a bit, and next there was some one whispered outside the door, and I very near laughed out loud, for I knew it was my father and mother that had got out of bed with the noise. 'Whatever is it?' says my mother. 'Hush! I don't know,' says my father, excited-like, 'don't disturb the boy. I hope he didn't hear nothing.'

"So, me knowing they were just outside, it made me bolder, and I slipped out of bed across to my little window—giving on the Close—but the dog he bored right down to the bottom of the bed—and I looked out. First go off I couldn't see anything. Then right down in the shadow under a buttress I made out what I shall always say was two spots of red—a dull red it was—nothing like a lamp or a fire, but just so as you could pick 'em out of the black shadow. I hadn't but just sighted 'em when it seemed we wasn't the only people that had been disturbed, because I see a window in a house on the left-hand side become lighted up, and the light moving. I just turned my head to make sure of it, and then looked back into the shadow for those two red things, and they were gone, and for all I peered about and stared, there was not a sign more of them. Then come my last fright that night—something come against my bare leg—but that was all right: that was my little dog had come out of bed, and prancing about, making a great to-do, only holding his tongue, and me seeing he was quite in spirits again, I took him back to bed and we slept the night out!

"Next morning I made out to tell my mother I'd had the dog in my room, and I was surprised, after all she'd said about it before, how quiet she took it. 'Did you?' she says. 'Well, by good rights you ought to go without your breakfast for doing such a thing behind my back: but I don't know as there's any great harm done, only another time you ask my permission, do you hear?' A bit after that I said something to my father about having heard the cats again. 'Cats,' he says, and he looked over at my poor mother, and she coughed and he says, 'Oh! ah! yes, cats. I believe I heard 'em myself.'

"That was a funny morning altogether: nothing seemed to go right. The organist he stopped in bed, and the minor Canon he forgot it was the 19th day and waited for the Venite; and after a bit the deputy he set off playing the chant for evensong, which was a minor; and then the Decani boys were laughing so much they couldn't sing, and when it came to the anthem the solo boy he got took with the giggles, and made out his nose was bleeding, and shoved the book at me what hadn't practised the verse and wasn't much of a singer if I had known it. Well, things was rougher, you see, fifty years ago, and I got a nip from the counter-tenor behind me that I remembered.

"So we got through somehow, and neither the men nor the boys weren't by way of waiting to see whether the Canon in residence—Mr. Henslow it was—would come to the vestries and fine 'em, but I don't believe he did: for one thing I fancy he'd read the wrong lesson for the first time in his life, and knew it. Anyhow Evans and me didn't find no difficulty in slipping up the stairs as I told you, and when we got up we laid ourselves down flat on our stomachs where we could just stretch our heads out over the old tomb, and we hadn't but just done so when we heard the verger that was then, first shutting the iron porch-gates and locking the south-west door, and then the transept door, so we knew there was something up, and they meant to keep the public out for a bit.

"Next thing was, the Dean and the Canon come in by their door on the north, and then I see my father, and old Palmer, and a couple of their best men, and Palmer stood a talking for a bit with the Dean in the middle of the choir. He had a coil of rope and the men had crows. All of 'em looked a bit nervous. So there they stood talking, and at last I heard the Dean say, 'Well, I've no time to waste, Palmer. If you think this'll satisfy Southminster people, I'll permit it to be done; but I must say this, that never in the whole course of my life have I heard such arrant nonsense from a practical man as I have from you. Don't you agree with me, Henslow?' As far as I could hear Mr. Henslow said something like 'Oh! well we're told, aren't we, Mr. Dean, not to judge others?' and the Dean he gave a kind of sniff, and walked straight up to the tomb, and took his stand behind it with his back to the screen, and the others they come edging up rather gingerly. Henslow, he stopped on the south side and scratched on his chin, he did. Then the Dean spoke up: 'Palmer,' he says, 'which can you do easiest, get the slab off the top, or shift one of the side slabs?'

"Old Palmer and his men they pottered about a bit looking round the edge of the top slab and sounding the sides on the south and east and west and everywhere but the north. Henslow said something about it being better to have a try at the south side, because there was more light and more room to move about in. Then my father, who'd been watching of them, went round to the north side, and knelt down and felt of the slab by the chink, and he got up and dusted his knees and says to the Dean: 'Beg pardon, Mr. Dean, but I think if Mr. Palmer'll try this here slab he'll find it'll come out easy enough. Seems to me one of the men could prize it out with his crow by means of this chink.' 'Ah! thank you, Worby,' says the Dean; 'that's a good suggestion. Palmer, let one of your men do that, will you?'

"So the man come round, and put his bar in and bore on it, and just that minute when they were all bending over, and we boys got our heads well out over the edge of the triforium, there come a most fearful crash down at the west end of the choir, as if a whole stack of big timber had fallen down a flight of stairs. Well, you can't expect me to tell you everything that happened all in a minute. Of course there was a terrible commotion. I heard the slab fall out, and the crowbar on the floor, and I heard the Dean say 'Good God!'

"When I looked down again I saw the Dean tumbled over on the floor, the men was making off down the choir, Henslow was just going to help the Dean up, Palmer was going to stop the men, as he said afterwards, and my father was sitting on the altar step with his face in his hands. The Dean he was very cross. 'I wish to goodness you'd look where you're coming to, Henslow,' he says. 'Why you should all take to your heels when a stick of wood tumbles down I cannot imagine,' and all Henslow could do, explaining he was right away on the other side of the tomb, would not satisfy him.

"Then Palmer came back and reported there was nothing to account for this noise and nothing seemingly fallen down, and when the Dean finished feeling of himself they gathered round—except my father, he sat where he was—and some one lighted up a bit of candle and they looked into the tomb. 'Nothing there,' says the Dean, 'what did I tell you? Stay! here's something. What's this: a bit of music paper, and a piece of torn stuff—part of a dress it looks like. Both quite modern—no interest whatever. Another time perhaps you'll take the advice of an educated man'—or something like that, and off he went, limping a bit, and out through the north door, only as he went he called back angry to Palmer for leaving the door standing open. Palmer called out 'Very sorry, sir,' but he shrugged his shoulders, and Henslow says, 'I fancy Mr. Dean's mistaken. I closed the door behind me, but he's a little upset.' Then Palmer says, 'Why, where's Worby?' and they saw him sitting on the step and went up to him. He was recovering himself, it seemed, and wiping his forehead, and Palmer helped him up on to his legs, as I was glad to see.

"They were too far off for me to hear what they said, but my father pointed to the north door in the aisle, and Palmer and Henslow both of them looked very surprised and scared. After a bit, my father and Henslow went out of the church, and the others made what haste they could to put the slab back and plaster it in. And about as the clock struck twelve the Cathedral was opened again and us boys made the best of our way home.

"I was in a great taking to know what it was had given my poor father such a turn, and when I got in and found him sitting in his chair taking a glass of spirits, and my mother standing looking anxious at him, I couldn't keep from bursting out and making confession where I'd been. But he didn't seem to take on, not in the way of losing his temper. 'You was there, was you? Well did you see it?' 'I see everything, father,' I said, 'except when the noise came.' 'Did you see what it was knocked the Dean over?' he says, 'that what come out of the monument? You didn't? Well, that's a mercy.' 'Why, what was it, father?' I said. 'Come, you must have seen it,' he says. 'Didn't you see? A thing like a man, all over hair, and two great eyes to it?'

"Well, that was all I could get out of him that time, and later on he seemed as if he was ashamed of being so frightened, and he used to put me off when I asked him about it. But years after, when I was got to be a grown man, we had more talk now and again on the matter, and he always said the same thing. 'Black it was,' he'd say, 'and a mass of hair, and two legs, and the light caught on its eyes.'

"Well, that's the tale of that tomb, Mr. Lake; it's one we don't tell to our visitors, and I should be obliged to you not to make any use of it till I'm out of the way. I doubt Mr. Evans'll feel the same as I do, if you ask him."

This proved to be the case. But over twenty years have passed by, and the grass is growing over both Worby and Evans; so Mr. Lake felt no difficulty about communicating his notes—taken in 1890—to me. He accompanied them with a sketch of the tomb and a copy of the short inscription on the metal cross which was affixed at the expense of Dr. Lyall to the centre of the northern side. It was from the Vulgate of Isaiah xxxiv., and consisted merely of the three words—

IBI CUBAVIT LAMIA.

# THE STORY OF A DISAPPEARANCE AND AN APPEARANCE

The letters which I now publish were sent to me recently by a person who knows me to be interested in ghost stories. There is no doubt about their authenticity. The paper on which they are written, the ink, and the whole external aspect put their date beyond the reach of question.

The only point which they do not make clear is the identity of the writer. He signs with initials only, and as none of the envelopes of the letters are preserved, the surname of his correspondent—obviously a married brother—is as obscure as his own. No further preliminary explanation is needed, I think. Luckily the first letter supplies all that could be expected.

## LETTER I

Great Chrishall, Dec. 22, 1837.

My Dear Robert,—It is with great regret for the enjoyment I am losing, and for a reason which you will deplore equally with myself, that I write to inform you that I am unable to join your circle for this Christmas: but you will agree with me that it is unavoidable when I say that I have within these few hours received a letter from Mrs. Hunt at B——, to the effect that our Uncle Henry has suddenly and mysteriously disappeared, and begging me to go down there immediately and join the search that is being made for him. Little as I, or you either, I think, have ever seen of Uncle, I naturally feel that this is not a request that can be regarded lightly, and accordingly I propose to go to B—— by this afternoon's mail, reaching it late in the evening. I shall not go to the Rectory, but put up at the King's Head, and to which you may address letters. I enclose a small draft, which you will please make use of for the benefit of the young people. I shall write you daily (supposing me to be detained more than a single day) what goes on, and you may be sure, should the business be cleared up in time to permit of my coming to the Manor after all, I shall present myself. I have but a few minutes at disposal. With cordial greetings to you all, and many regrets, believe me, your affectionate Bro.,

W. R.

## LETTER II

King's Head, Dec. 23, '37.

My Dear Robert,—In the first place, there is as yet no news of Uncle H., and I think you may finally dismiss any idea—I won't say hope—that I might after all "turn up" for Xmas. However, my thoughts will be with you, and you have my best wishes for a really festive day. Mind that none of my nephews or nieces expend any fraction of their guineas on presents for me.

Since I got here I have been blaming myself for taking this affair of Uncle H. too easily. From what people here say, I gather that there is very little hope that he can still be alive; but whether it is accident or design that carried him off I cannot judge. The facts are these. On Friday the 19th, he went as usual shortly before five o'clock to read evening prayers at the Church; and when they were over the clerk brought him a message, in response to which he set off to pay a visit to a sick person at an outlying cottage the better part of two miles away. He paid the visit, and started on his return journey at about half-past six. This is the last that is known of him. The people here are very much grieved at his loss; he had been here many years, as you know, and though, as you also know, he was not the most genial of men, and had more than a little of the martinet in his composition, he seems to have been active in good works, and unsparing of trouble to himself.

Poor Mrs. Hunt, who has been his housekeeper ever since she left Woodley, is quite overcome: it seems like the end of the world to her. I am glad that I did not entertain the idea of taking quarters at the Rectory; and I have declined several kindly offers of hospitality from people in the place, preferring as I do to be independent, and finding myself very comfortable here.

You will, of course, wish to know what has been done in the way of inquiry and search. First, nothing was to be expected from investigation at the Rectory; and to be brief, nothing has transpired. I asked Mrs. Hunt—as others had done before—whether there was either any unfavourable symptom in her master such as might portend a sudden stroke, or attack of illness, or whether he had ever had reason to apprehend any such thing: but both she, and also his medical man, were clear that this was not the case. He was quite in his usual health. In the second place, naturally, ponds and streams have been dragged, and fields in the neighbourhood which he is known to have visited last, have been searched—without result. I have myself talked to the parish clerk and—more important—have been to the house where he paid his visit.

There can be no question of any foul play on these people's part. The one man in the house is ill in bed and very weak: the wife and the children of course could do nothing themselves, nor is there the shadow of a probability that they or any of them should have agreed to decoy poor Uncle H. out in order that he might be attacked on the way back. They had told what they knew to several other inquirers already, but the woman repeated it to me. The Rector was looking just as usual: he wasn't very long with the sick man—"He ain't," she said, "like some what has a gift in prayer; but there, if we was all that way, 'owever would the chapel people get their living?" He left some money when he went away, and one of the children saw him cross the stile into the next field. He was dressed as he always was: wore his bands—I gather he is nearly the last man remaining who does so—at any rate in this district.

You see I am putting down everything. The fact is that I have nothing else to do, having brought no business papers with me; and, moreover, it serves to clear my own mind, and may suggest points which have been overlooked. So I shall continue to write all that passes, even to conversations if need be—you may read or not as you please, but pray keep the letters. I have another reason for writing so fully, but it is not a very tangible one.

You may ask if I have myself made any search in the fields near the cottage. Something—a good deal—has been done by others, as I mentioned; but I hope to go over the ground to-morrow. Bow Street has now been informed, and will send down by to-night's coach, but I do not think they will make much of the job. There is no snow, which might have helped us. The fields are all grass. Of course I was on the qui vive for any indication to-day both going and returning;

but there was a thick mist on the way back, and I was not in trim for wandering about unknown pastures, especially on an evening when bushes looked like men, and a cow lowing in the distance might have been the last trump. I assure you, if Uncle Henry had stepped out from among the trees in a little copse which borders the path at one place, carrying his head under his arm, I should have been very little more uncomfortable than I was. To tell you the truth, I was rather expecting something of the kind. But I must drop my pen for the moment: Mr. Lucas, the curate, is announced.

Later. Mr. Lucas has been, and gone, and there is not much beyond the decencies of ordinary sentiment to be got from him. I can see that he has given up any idea that the Rector can be alive, and that, so far as he can be, he is truly sorry. I can also discern that even in a more emotional person than Mr. Lucas, Uncle Henry was not likely to inspire strong attachment.

Besides Mr. Lucas, I have had another visitor in the shape of my Boniface—mine host of the "King's Head"—who came to see whether I had everything I wished, and who really requires the pen of a Boz to do him justice. He was very solemn and weighty at first. "Well, sir," he said, "I suppose we must bow our 'ead beneath the blow, as my poor wife had used to say. So far as I can gather there's been neither hide nor yet hair of our late respected incumbent scented out as yet; not that he was what the Scripture terms a hairy man in any sense of the word."

I said—as well as I could—that I supposed not, but could not help adding that I had heard he was sometimes a little difficult to deal with. Mr. Bowman looked at me sharply for a moment, and then passed in a flash from solemn sympathy to impassioned declamation. "When I think," he said, "of the language that man see fit to employ to me in this here parlour over no more a matter than a cask of beer—such a thing as I told him might happen any day of the week to a man with a family—though as it turned out he was quite under a mistake, and that I knew at the time, only I was that shocked to hear him I couldn't lay my tongue to the right expression."

He stopped abruptly and eyed me with some embarrassment. I only said, "Dear me, I'm sorry to hear you had any little differences; I suppose my uncle will be a good deal missed in the parish?" Mr. Bowman drew a long breath. "Ah, yes!" he said; "your uncle! You'll understand me when I say that for the moment it had slipped my remembrance that he was a relative; and natural enough, I must say, as it should, for as to you bearing any resemblance to—to him, the notion of any such a thing is clean ridiculous. All the same, 'ad I 'ave bore it in my mind, you'll be among the first to feel, I'm sure, as I should have abstained my lips, or rather I should not have abstained my lips with no such reflections."

I assured him that I quite understood, and was going to have asked him some further questions, but he was called away to see after some business. By the way, you need not take it into your head that he has anything to fear from the inquiry into poor Uncle Henry's disappearance—though, no doubt, in the watches of the night it will occur to him that I think he has, and I may expect explanations to-morrow.

I must close this letter: it has to go by the late coach.

## LETTER III

Dec. 25, '37.

My Dear Robert,—This is a curious letter to be writing on Christmas Day, and yet after all there is nothing much in it. Or there may be—you shall be the judge. At least, nothing decisive. The Bow Street men practically say that they have no clue. The length of time and the weather conditions have made all tracks so faint as to be quite useless: nothing that belonged to the dead man—I'm afraid no other word will do—has been picked up.

As I expected, Mr. Bowman was uneasy in his mind this morning; quite early I heard him holding forth in a very distinct voice—purposely so, I thought—to the Bow Street officers in the bar, as to the loss that the town had sustained in their Rector, and as to the necessity of leaving no stone unturned (he was very great on this phrase) in order to come at the truth. I suspect him of being an orator of repute at convivial meetings.

When I was at breakfast he came to wait on me, and took an opportunity when handing a muffin to say in a low tone, "I 'ope, sir, you reconize as my feelings towards your relative is not actuated by any taint of what you may call melignity—you can leave the room, Eliza, I will see the gentleman 'as all he requires with my own hands—I ask your pardon, sir, but you must be well aware a man is not always master of himself: and when that man has been 'urt in his mind by the application of expressions which I will go so far as to say 'ad not ought to have been made use of (his voice was rising all this time and his face growing redder); no, sir; and 'ere, if you will permit of it, I should like to explain to you in a very few words the exact state of the bone of contention. This cask—I might more truly call it a firkin—of beer—"

I felt it was time to interpose, and said that I did not see that it would help us very much to go into that matter in detail. Mr. Bowman acquiesced, and resumed more calmly:

"Well, sir, I bow to your ruling, and as you say, be that here or be it there, it don't contribute a great deal, perhaps, to the present question. All I wish you to understand is that I am prepared as you are yourself to lend every hand to the business we have afore us, and—as I took the opportunity to say as much to the Orficers not three-quarters of an hour ago—to leave no stone unturned as may throw even a spark of light on this painful matter."

In fact, Mr. Bowman did accompany us on our exploration, but though I am sure his genuine wish was to be helpful, I am afraid he did not contribute to the serious side of it. He appeared to be under the impression that we were likely to meet either Uncle Henry or the person responsible for his disappearance, walking about the fields—and did a great deal of shading his eyes with his hand and calling our attention, by pointing with his stick, to distant cattle and labourers. He held several long conversations with old women whom we met, and was very strict and severe in his manner—but on each occasion returned to our party saying, "Well, I find she don't seem to 'ave no connexion with this sad affair. I think you may take it from me, sir, as there's little or no light to be looked for from that quarter; not without she's keeping somethink back intentional."

We gained no appreciable result, as I told you at starting; the Bow Street men have left the town, whether for London or not, I am not sure.

This evening I had company in the shape of a bagman, a smartish fellow. He knew what was going forward, but though he has been on the roads for some days about here, he had nothing to tell of suspicious characters—tramps, wandering sailors or gipsies. He was very full of a capital Punch and Judy Show he had seen this same day at W——, and asked if it had been here yet, and advised me by no means to miss it if it does come. The best Punch and the best Toby dog, he said, he had ever come across. Toby dogs, you know, are the last new thing in the shows. I have only seen one myself, but before long all the men will have them.

Now why, you will want to know, do I trouble to write all this to you? I am obliged to do it, because it has something to do with another absurd trifle (as you will inevitably say), which in my present state of rather unquiet fancy—nothing more, perhaps—I have to put down. It is a dream, sir, which I am going to record, and I must say it is one of the oddest I have had. Is there anything in it beyond what the bagman's talk and Uncle Henry's disappearance could have suggested? You, I repeat, shall judge: I am not in a sufficiently cool and judicial frame to do so.

It began with what I can only describe as a pulling aside of curtains: and I found myself seated in a place—I don't know whether in doors or out. There were people—only a few—on either side of me, but I did not recognize them, or indeed think much about them. They never spoke, but, so far as I remember, were all grave and pale-faced and looked fixedly before them. Facing me there was a Punch and Judy Show, perhaps rather larger than the ordinary ones, painted with black figures on a reddish-yellow ground. Behind it and on each side was only darkness, but in front there was a sufficiency of light. I was "strung up" to a high degree of expectation and listened every moment to hear the panpipes and the Roo-too-too-it. Instead of that there came suddenly an enormous—I can use no other word—an enormous single toll of a bell, I don't know from how far off—somewhere behind. The little curtain flew up and the drama began.

I believe someone once tried to re-write Punch as a serious tragedy; but whoever he may have been, this performance would have suited him exactly. There was something Satanic about the hero. He varied his methods of attack: for some of his victims he lay in wait, and to see his horrible face—it was yellowish white, I may remark—peering round the wings made me think of the Vampyre in Fuseli's foul sketch. To others he was polite and carneying—particularly to the unfortunate alien who can only say Shallabalah—though what Punch said I never could catch. But with all of them I came to dread the moment of death. The crack of the stick on their skulls, which in the ordinary way delights me, had here a crushing sound as if the bone was giving way, and the victims quivered and kicked as they lay. The baby—it sounds more ridiculous as I go on—the baby, I am sure, was alive. Punch wrung its neck, and if the choke or squeak which it gave were not real, I know nothing of reality.

The stage got perceptibly darker as each crime was consummated, and at last there was one murder which was done quite in the dark, so that I could see nothing of the victim, and took some time to effect. It was accompanied by hard breathing and horrid muffled sounds, and after it Punch came and sat on the foot-board and fanned himself and looked at his shoes, which were bloody, and hung his head on one side, and sniggered in so deadly a fashion that I saw some of those beside me cover their faces, and I would gladly have done the same. But in the meantime the scene behind Punch was clearing, and showed, not the usual house front, but something more ambitious—a grove of trees and the gentle slope of a hill, with a very natural—in fact, I should say a real—moon shining on it. Over this there rose slowly an object which I soon perceived to be a human figure with something peculiar about the head—what, I was unable at first to see. It did not stand on its feet, but began creeping or dragging itself across the middle distance towards Punch, who still sat back to it; and by this time, I may remark (though it did not occur to me at the moment) that all pretence of this being a puppet show had vanished. Punch was still Punch, it is true, but, like the others, was in some sense a live creature, and both moved themselves at their own will.

When I next glanced at him he was sitting in malignant reflection; but in another instant something seemed to attract his attention, and he first sat up sharply and then turned round, and evidently caught sight of the person that was approaching him and was in fact now very near. Then, indeed, did he show unmistakable signs of terror: catching up his stick, he rushed towards the wood, only just eluding the arm of his pursuer, which was suddenly flung out to intercept him. It was with a revulsion which I cannot easily express that I now saw more or less clearly what this pursuer was like. He was a sturdy figure clad in black, and, as I thought, wearing bands: his head was covered with a whitish bag.

The chase which now began lasted I do not know how long, now among the trees, now along the slope of the field, sometimes both figures disappearing wholly for a few seconds, and only some uncertain sounds letting one know that they were still afoot. At length there came a moment when Punch, evidently exhausted, staggered in from the left and threw himself down among the trees. His pursuer was not long after him, and came looking uncertainly from side to side. Then, catching sight of the figure on the ground, he too threw himself down—his back was turned to the audience—with a swift motion twitched the covering from his head, and thrust his face into that of Punch. Everything on the instant grew dark.

There was one long, loud, shuddering scream, and I awoke to find myself looking straight into the face of—what in all the world do you think?—but a large owl, which was seated on my window-sill immediately opposite my bed-foot, holding up its wings like two shrouded arms. I caught the fierce glance of its yellow eyes, and then it was gone. I heard the single enormous bell again—very likely, as you are saying to yourself, the church clock; but I do not think so—and then I was broad awake.

All this, I may say, happened within the last half-hour. There was no probability of my getting to sleep again, so I got up, put on clothes enough to keep me warm, and am writing this rigmarole in the first hours of Christmas Day. Have I left out anything? Yes, there was no Toby dog, and the names over the front of the Punch and Judy booth were Kidman and Gallop, which were certainly not what the bagman told me to look out for.

By this time, I feel a little more as if I could sleep, so this shall be sealed and wafered.

## LETTER IV

Dec. 26, '37.

My Dear Robert,—All is over. The body has been found. I do not make excuses for not having sent off my news by last night's mail, for the simple reason that I was incapable of putting pen to paper. The events that attended the discovery bewildered me so completely that I needed what I could get of a night's rest to enable me to face the situation at all. Now I can give you my journal of the day, certainly the strangest Christmas Day that ever I spent or am likely to spend.

The first incident was not very serious. Mr. Bowman had, I think, been keeping Christmas Eve, and was a little inclined to be captious: at least, he was not on foot very early, and to judge from what I could hear, neither men or maids could do anything to please him. The latter were certainly reduced to tears; nor am I sure that Mr. Bowman succeeded in preserving a manly composure. At any rate, when I came downstairs, it was in a broken voice that he wished me the compliments of the season, and a little later on, when he paid his visit of ceremony at breakfast, he was far from cheerful: even Byronic, I might almost say, in his outlook on life.

"I don't know," he said, "if you think with me, sir; but every Christmas as comes round the world seems a hollerer thing to me. Why, take an example now from what lays under my own eye. There's my servant Eliza—been with me now for going on fifteen years. I thought I could have placed my confidence in Elizar, and yet this very morning—Christmas morning too, of all the blessed days in the year—with the bells a ringing and—and—all like that—I say, this very morning, had it not have been for Providence watching over us all, that girl would have put—indeed I may go so far to say, 'ad put the cheese on your breakfast table——" He saw I was about to speak, and waved his hand at me. "It's all very well for you to say, 'Yes, Mr. Bowman, but you took away the cheese and locked it up in the cupboard,' which I did, and have the key here, or if not the actual key one very much about the same size. That's true enough, sir, but what do you think is the effect of that action on me? Why it's no exaggeration for me to say that the ground is cut from under my feet. And yet when I said as much to Eliza, not nasty, mind you, but just firm like, what was my return? 'Oh,' she says: 'Well,' she says, 'there wasn't no bones broke, I suppose.' Well, sir, it 'urt me, that's all I can say: it 'urt me, and I don't like to think of it now."

There was an ominous pause here, in which I ventured to say something like, "Yes, very trying," and then asked at what hour the church service was to be. "Eleven o'clock," Mr. Bowman said with a heavy sigh. "Ah, you won't have no such discourse from poor Mr. Lucas as what you would have done from our late Rector. Him and me may have had our little differences, and did do, more's the pity."

I could see that a powerful effort was needed to keep him off the vexed question of the cask of beer, but he made it. "But I will say this, that a better preacher, nor yet one to stand faster by his rights, or what he considered to be his rights—however, that's not the question now—I for one, never set under. Some might say, 'Was he a eloquent man?' and to that my answer would be: 'Well, there you've a better right per'aps to speak of your own uncle than what I have.' Others might ask, 'Did he keep a hold of his congregation?' and there again I should reply, 'That depends.' But as I say—Yes, Eliza, my girl, I'm coming—eleven o'clock, sir, and you inquire for the King's Head pew." I believe Eliza had been very near the door, and shall consider it in my vail.

The next episode was church: I felt Mr. Lucas had a difficult task in doing justice to Christmas sentiments, and also to the feeling of disquiet and regret which, whatever Mr. Bowman might say, was clearly prevalent. I do not think he rose to the occasion. I was uncomfortable. The organ wolved—you know what I mean: the wind died—twice in the Christmas Hymn, and the tenor bell, I suppose owing to some negligence on the part of the ringers, kept sounding faintly about once in a minute during the sermon. The clerk sent up a man to see to it, but he seemed unable to do much. I was glad when it was over. There was an odd incident, too, before the service. I went in rather early, and came upon two men carrying the parish bier back to its place under the tower. From what I overheard them saying, it appeared that it had been put out by mistake, by some one who was not there. I also saw the clerk busy folding up a moth-eaten velvet pall—not a sight for Christmas Day.

I dined soon after this, and then, feeling disinclined to go out, took my seat by the fire in the parlour, with the last number of Pickwick, which I had been saving up for some days. I thought I could be sure of keeping awake over this, but I turned out as bad as our friend Smith. I suppose it was half-past two when I was roused by a piercing whistle and laughing and talking voices outside in the market-place. It was a Punch and Judy—I had no doubt the one that my bagman had seen at W——. I was half delighted, half not—the latter because my unpleasant dream came back to me so vividly; but, anyhow, I determined to see it through, and I sent Eliza out with a crown-piece to the performers and a request that they would face my window if they could manage it.

The show was a very smart new one; the names of the proprietors, I need hardly tell you, were Italian, Foresta and Calpigi. The Toby dog was there, as I had been led to expect. All B—— turned out, but did not obstruct my view, for I was at the large first-floor window and not ten yards away.

The play began on the stroke of a quarter to three by the church clock. Certainly it was very good; and I was soon relieved to find that the disgust my dream had given me for Punch's onslaughts on his ill-starred visitors was only transient. I laughed at the demise of the Turncock, the Foreigner, the Beadle, and even the baby. The only drawback was the Toby dog's developing a tendency to howl in the wrong place. Something had occurred, I suppose, to upset him, and something considerable: for, I forget exactly at what point, he gave a most lamentable cry, leapt off the foot board, and shot away across the market-place and down a side street. There was a stage-wait, but only a brief one. I suppose the men decided that it was no good going after him, and that he was likely to turn up again at night.

We went on. Punch dealt faithfully with Judy, and in fact with all comers; and then came the moment when the gallows was erected, and the great scene with Mr. Ketch was to be enacted. It was now that something happened of which I can certainly not yet see the import fully. You have witnessed an execution, and know what the criminal's head looks like with the cap on. If you are like me, you never wish to think of it again, and I do not willingly remind you of it. It was just such a head as that, that I, from my somewhat higher post, saw in the inside of the show-box; but at first the audience did not see it. I expected it to emerge into their view, but instead of that there slowly rose for a few seconds an uncovered face, with an expression of terror upon it, of which I have never imagined the like. It seemed as if the man, whoever he was, was being forcibly lifted, with his arms somehow pinioned or held back, towards the little gibbet on the stage. I could just see the nightcapped head behind him. Then there was a cry and a crash. The whole show-box fell over backwards; kicking legs were seen among the ruins, and then two figures—as some said; I can only answer for one—were visible running at top speed across the square and disappearing in a lane which leads to the fields.

Of course everybody gave chase. I followed; but the pace was killing, and very few were in, literally, at the death. It happened in a chalk pit: the man went over the edge quite blindly and broke his neck. They searched everywhere for the other, until it occurred to me to ask whether he had ever left the market-place. At first everyone was sure that he had; but when we came to look, he was there, under the show-box, dead too.

But in the chalk pit it was that poor Uncle Henry's body was found, with a sack over the head, the throat horribly mangled. It was a peaked corner of the sack sticking out of the soil that attracted attention. I cannot bring myself to write in greater detail.

I forgot to say the men's real names were Kidman and Gallop. I feel sure I have heard them, but no one here seems to know anything about them.

I am coming to you as soon as I can after the funeral. I must tell you when we meet what I think of it all.

# TWO DOCTORS

It is a very common thing, in my experience, to find papers shut up in old books; but one of the rarest things to come across any such that are at all interesting. Still it does happen, and one should never destroy them unlooked at. Now it was a practice of mine before the war occasionally to buy old ledgers of which the paper was good, and which possessed a good many blank leaves, and to extract these and use them for my own notes and writings. One such I purchased for a small sum in 1911. It was tightly clasped, and its boards were warped by having for years been obliged to embrace a number of extraneous sheets. Three-quarters of this inserted matter had lost all vestige of importance for any living human being: one bundle had not. That it belonged to a lawyer is certain, for it is endorsed: The strangest case I have yet met, and bears initials, and an address in Gray's Inn. It is only materials for a case, and consists of statements by possible witnesses. The man who would have been the defendant or prisoner seems never to have appeared. The dossier is not complete, but, such as it is, it furnishes a riddle in which the supernatural appears to play a part. You must see what you can make of it.

The following is the setting and the tale as I elicit it.

Dr. Abell was walking in his garden one afternoon waiting for his horse to be brought round that he might set out on his visits for the day. As the place was Islington, the month June, and the year 1718, we conceive the surroundings as being countrified and pleasant. To him entered his confidential servant, Luke Jennett, who had been with him twenty years.

"I said I wished to speak to him, and what I had to say might take some quarter of an hour. He accordingly bade me go into his study, which was a room opening on the terrace path where he was walking, and came in himself and sat down. I told him that, much against my will, I must look out for another place. He inquired what was my reason, in consideration I had been so long with him. I said if he would excuse me he would do me a great kindness, because (this appears to have been common form even in 1718) I was one that always liked to have everything pleasant about me. As well as I can remember, he said that was his case likewise, but he would wish to know why I should change my mind after so many years, and, says he, 'you know there can be no talk of a remembrance of you in my will if you leave my service now.' I said I had made my reckoning of that.

"'Then,' says he, 'you must have some complaint to make, and if I could I would willingly set it right.' And at that I told him, not seeing how I could keep it back, the matter of my former affidavit and of the bedstaff in the dispensing-room, and said that a house where such things happened was no place for me. At which he, looking very black upon me, said no more, but called me fool, and said he would pay what was owing me in the morning; and so, his horse being waiting, went out. So for that night I lodged with my sister's husband near Battle Bridge and came early next morning to my late master, who then made a great matter that I had not lain in his house and stopped a crown out of my wages owing.

"After that I took service here and there, not for long at a time, and saw no more of him till I came to be Dr. Quinn's man at Dodds Hall in Islington."

There is one very obscure part in this statement, namely, the reference to the former affidavit and the matter of the bedstaff. The former affidavit is not in the bundle of papers. It is to be feared that it was taken out to be read because of its special oddity, and not put back. Of what nature the story was may be guessed later, but as yet no clue has been put into our hands.

The Rector of Islington, Jonathan Pratt, is the next to step forward. He furnishes particulars of the standing and reputation of Dr. Abell and Dr. Quinn, both of whom lived and practised in his parish.

"It is not to be supposed," he says, "that a physician should be a regular attendant at morning and evening prayers, or at the Wednesday lectures, but within the measure of their ability I would say that both these persons fulfilled their obligations as loyal members of the Church of England. At the same time (as you desire my private mind) I must say, in the language of the schools, distinguo. Dr. A. was to me a source of perplexity, Dr. Q. to my eye a plain, honest believer, not inquiring over closely into points of belief, but squaring his practice to what lights he had. The other interested himself in questions to which Providence, as I hold, designs no answer to be given us in this state: he would ask me, for example, what place I believed those beings now to hold in the scheme of creation which by some are thought neither to have stood fast when the rebel angels fell, nor to have joined with them to the full pitch of their transgression.

"As was suitable, my first answer to him was a question, What warrant he had for supposing any such beings to exist? for that there was none in Scripture I took it he was aware. It appeared—for as I am on the subject, the whole tale may be given—that he grounded himself on such passages as that of the satyr which Jerome tells us conversed with Antony; but thought too that some parts of Scripture might be cited in support. 'And besides,' said he, 'you know 'tis the universal belief among those that spend their days and nights abroad, and I would add that if your calling took you so continuously as it does me about the country lanes by night, you might not be so surprised as I see you to be by my suggestion.' 'You are then of John Milton's mind,' I said, 'and hold that

> *Millions of spiritual creatures walk the earth*
> *Unseen, both when we wake and when we sleep.'*

"'I do not know,' he said, 'why Milton should take upon himself to say "unseen"; though to be sure he was blind when he wrote that. But for the rest, why, yes, I think he was in the right.' 'Well,' I said, 'though not so often as you, I am not seldom called abroad pretty late; but I have no mind of meeting a satyr in our Islington lanes in all the years I have been here; and if you have had the better luck, I am sure the Royal Society would be glad to know of it.'

"I am reminded of these trifling expressions because Dr. A. took them so ill, stamping out of the room in a huff with some such word as that these high and dry parsons had no eyes but for a prayerbook or a pint of wine.

"But this was not the only time that our conversation took a remarkable turn. There was an evening when he came in, at first seeming gay and in good spirits, but afterwards as he sat and smoked by the fire falling into a musing way; out of which to rouse him I said pleasantly that I supposed he had had no meetings of late with his odd friends. A question which did effectually arouse him, for he looked most wildly, and as if scared, upon me, and said, 'You were never there? I did not see you. Who brought you?' And then in a more collected tone, 'What was this about a meeting? I believe I must have been in a doze.' To which I answered that I was thinking of fauns and centaurs in the dark lane, and not of a witches' Sabbath; but it seemed he took it differently.

"'Well,' said he, 'I can plead guilty to neither; but I find you very much more of a sceptic than becomes your cloth. If you care to know about the dark lane you might do worse than ask my housekeeper that lived at the other end of it when she was a child.' 'Yes,' said I, 'and the old women in the almshouse and the children in the kennel. If I were you, I would send to your brother Quinn for a bolus to clear your brain.' 'Damn Quinn,' says he; 'talk no more of him: he has embezzled four of my best patients this month; I believe it is that cursed man of his, Jennett, that used to be with me, his tongue is never still; it should be nailed to the pillory if he had his deserts.' This, I may say, was the only time of his showing me that he had any grudge against either Dr. Quinn or Jennett, and as was my business, I did my best to persuade him he was mistaken in them. Yet it could not be denied that some respectable families in the parish had given him the cold shoulder, and for no reason that they were willing to allege. The end was that he said he had not done so ill at Islington but that he could afford to live at ease elsewhere when he chose, and anyhow he bore Dr. Quinn no malice. I think I now remember what observation of mine drew him into the train of thought which he next pursued. It was, I believe, my mentioning some juggling tricks which my brother in the East Indies had seen at the court of the Rajah of Mysore. 'A convenient thing enough,' said Dr. Abell to me, 'if by some arrangement a man could get the power of communicating motion and energy to inanimate objects.' 'As if the axe should move itself against him that lifts it; something of that kind?' 'Well, I don't know that that was in my mind so much; but if you could summon such a volume from your shelf or even order it to open at the right page.'

"He was sitting by the fire—it was a cold evening—and stretched out his hand that way, and just then the fire-irons, or at least the poker, fell over towards him with a great clatter, and I did not hear what else he said. But I told him that I could not easily conceive of an arrangement, as he called it, of such a kind that would not include as one of its conditions a heavier payment than any Christian would care to make; to which he assented. 'But,' he said, 'I have no doubt these bargains can be made very tempting, very persuasive. Still, you would not favour them, eh, Doctor? No, I suppose not.'

"This is as much as I know of Dr. Abell's mind, and the feeling between these men. Dr. Quinn, as I said, was a plain, honest creature, and a man to whom I would have gone—indeed I have before now gone to him for advice on matters of business. He was, however, every now and again, and particularly of late, not exempt from troublesome fancies. There was certainly a time when he was so much harassed by his dreams that he could not keep them to himself, but would tell them to his acquaintances and among them to me. I was at supper at his house, and he was not inclined to let me leave him at my usual time. 'If you go,' he said, 'there will be nothing for it but I must go to bed and dream of the chrysalis.' 'You might be worse off,' said I. 'I do not think it,' he said, and he shook himself like a man who is displeased with the complexion of his thoughts. 'I only meant,' said I, 'that a chrysalis is an innocent thing.' 'This one is not,' he said, 'and I do not care to think of it.'

"However, sooner than lose my company he was fain to tell me (for I pressed him) that this was a dream which had come to him several times of late, and even more than once in a night. It was to this effect, that he seemed to himself to wake under an extreme compulsion to rise and go out of doors. So he would dress himself and go down to his garden door. By the door there stood a spade which he must take, and go out into the garden, and at a particular place in the shrubbery somewhat clear and upon which the moon shone, for there was always in his dream a full moon, he would feel himself forced to dig. And after some time the spade would uncover something light-coloured, which he would perceive to be a stuff, linen or woollen, and this he must clear with his hands. It was always the same: of the size of a man and shaped like the chrysalis of a moth, with the folds showing a promise of an opening at one end.

"He could not describe how gladly he would have left all at this stage and run to the house, but he must not escape so easily. So with many groans, and knowing only too well what to expect, he parted these folds of stuff, or, as it sometimes seemed to be, membrane, and disclosed a head covered with a smooth pink skin, which breaking as the creature stirred, showed him his own face in a state of death. The telling of this so much disturbed him that I was forced out of mere compassion to sit with him the greater part of the night and talk with him upon indifferent subjects. He said that upon every recurrence of this dream he woke and found himself, as it were, fighting for his breath."

Another extract from Luke Jennett's long continuous statement comes in at this point.

"I never told tales of my master, Dr. Abell, to anybody in the neighbourhood. When I was in another service I remember to have spoken to my fellow-servants about the matter of the bedstaff, but I am sure I never said either I or he were the persons concerned, and it met with so little credit that I was affronted and thought best to keep it to myself. And when I came back to Islington and found Dr. Abell still there, who I was told had left the parish, I was clear that it behoved me to use great discretion, for indeed I was afraid of the man, and it is certain I was no party to spreading any ill report of him. My master, Dr. Quinn, was a very just, honest man, and no maker of mischief. I am sure he never stirred a finger nor said a word by way of inducement to a soul to make them leave going to Dr. Abell and come to him; nay, he would hardly be persuaded to attend them that came, until he was convinced that if he did not they would send into the town for a physician rather than do as they had hitherto done.

"I believe it may be proved that Dr. Abell came into my master's house more than once. We had a new chambermaid out of Hertfordshire, and she asked me who was the gentleman that was looking after the master, that is Dr. Quinn, when he was out, and seemed so disappointed that he was out. She said whoever he was he knew the way of the house well, running at once into the study and then into the dispensing-room, and last into the bed-chamber. I made her tell me what he was like, and what she said was suitable enough to Dr. Abell; but besides she told me she saw the same man at church and some one told her that was the Doctor.

"It was just after this that my master began to have his bad nights, and complained to me and other persons, and in particular what discomfort he suffered from his pillow and bedclothes. He said he must buy some to suit him, and should do his own marketing. And accordingly brought home a parcel which he said was of the right quality, but where he bought it we had then no knowledge, only they were marked in thread with a coronet and a bird. The women said they were of a sort not commonly met with and very fine, and my master said they were the comfortablest he ever used, and he slept now both soft and deep. Also the feather pillows were the best sorted and his head would sink into them as if they were a cloud: which I have myself remarked several times when I came to wake him of a morning, his face being almost hid by the pillow closing over it.

"I had never any communication with Dr. Abell after I came back to Islington, but one day when he passed me in the street and asked me whether I was not looking for another service, to which I answered I was very well suited where I was, but he said I was a tickle-minded fellow and he doubted not he should soon hear I was on the world again, which indeed proved true."

Dr. Pratt is next taken up where he left off.

"On the 16th I was called up out of my bed soon after it was light—that is about five—with a message that Dr. Quinn was dead or dying. Making my way to his house I found there was no doubt which was the truth. All the persons in the house except the one that let me in were already in his chamber and standing about his bed, but none touching him. He was stretched in the midst of the bed, on his back, without any disorder, and indeed had the appearance of one ready laid out for burial. His hands, I think, were even crossed on his breast. The only thing not usual was that nothing was to be seen of his face, the two ends of the pillow or bolster appearing to be closed quite over it. These I immediately pulled apart, at the same time rebuking those present, and especially the man, for not at once coming to the assistance of his master. He, however, only looked at me and shook his head, having evidently no more hope than myself that there was anything but a corpse before us.

"Indeed it was plain to any one possessed of the least experience that he was not only dead, but had died of suffocation. Nor could it be conceived that his death was accidentally caused by the mere folding of the pillow over his face. How should he not, feeling the oppression, have lifted his hands to put it away? whereas not a fold of the sheet which was closely gathered about him, as I now observed, was disordered. The next thing was to procure a physician. I had bethought me of this on leaving my house, and sent on the messenger who had come to me to Dr. Abell; but I now heard that he was away from home, and the nearest surgeon was got, who however could tell no more, at least without opening the body, than we already knew.

"As to any person entering the room with evil purpose (which was the next point to be cleared), it was visible that the bolts of the door were burst from their stanchions, and the stanchions broken away from the door-post by main force; and there was a sufficient body of witness, the smith among them, to testify that this had been done but a few minutes before I came. The chamber being moreover at the top of the house, the window was neither easy of access nor did it show any sign of an exit made that way, either by marks upon the sill or footprints below upon soft mould."

The surgeon's evidence forms of course part of the report of the inquest, but since it has nothing but remarks upon the healthy state of the larger organs and the coagulation of blood in various parts of the body, it need not be reproduced. The verdict was "Death by the visitation of God."

Annexed to the other papers is one which I was at first inclined to suppose had made its way among them by mistake. Upon further consideration I think I can divine a reason for its presence.

It relates to the rifling of a mausoleum in Middlesex which stood in a park (now broken up), the property of a noble family which I will not name. The outrage was not that of an ordinary resurrection man. The object, it seemed likely, was theft. The account is blunt and terrible. I shall not quote it. A dealer in the North of London suffered heavy penalties as a receiver of stolen goods in connexion with the affair.

www.ingramcontent.com/pod-product-compliance
Lightning Source LLC
Chambersburg PA
CBHW011513170626
46810CB00009B/3342

* 9 7 8 1 6 3 6 3 7 2 7 8 5 *